MY FATHER
IS A HERO

MY FATHER IS A HERO

Nishant Kaushik

Srishti
PUBLISHERS & DISTRIBUTORS

SRISHTI PUBLISHERS & DISTRIBUTORS
Registered Office: N-16, C.R. Park
New Delhi – 110 019
Corporate Office: 212A, Peacock Lane
Shahpur Jat, New Delhi – 110 049
editorial@srishtipublishers.com

First published by
Srishti Publishers & Distributors in 2016

Acknowledgements

This book is a token of respect towards every father who has been a hero to his child. On top of this list of fathers is my own.

I must hence first thank my parents, not just for inspiring me to write this story, but also for teaching me values that have been invaluable in shaping my life.

Kamini, for systematically critiquing my work (my manuscript as well as my habits in general), and for always being around.

My sisters and their beautiful families, my wonderfully supportive in-laws, thank you for the encouragement even when I had not, in the strictest sense, earned it.

Tarun Tripathi and Vinit Bharucha, for the opportunity I got to work with them and for their creative inputs.

My publishers, for their faith in my work when it mattered the most; the entire editorial team for their tireless sincerity in working with me on the manuscript with a discipline that I could do well to be motivated by.

But most importantly, Kayaan: for being just the most amazing son in the world. I hope you get to be as proud of your father as I am of mine.

The circle of life

'Raja Ram Mohan Roy.'

'Incorrect. Try again.'

'I am quite sure it is.'

'I am sure it is not.'

Vaibhav stole a quick glance at his daughter through the side mirror of his 2006 Splendor. He observed her with adoration as he often did; today, through the smog rising in the city air. She had caramel eyes, big and round. Her hair was naturally wavy and fell perfectly over her little shoulders. Nisha was a beautiful girl, which meant that she looked nothing like her father. Vaibhav was, by no stretch of imagination, a good-looking man. His fair excuse could have been that he hardly had the time or motivation to stand before a mirror and work on his appearance. But then he was not a particularly charming prince even when he was eighteen and had more time on hand. Today, he was vaguely aware that his hair always housed more oil than it needed to. There was always a row of sweat beads shining above his moustache. His skin was patchy and rough. And his teeth were very white, but they took up too much

1

screen space on his face. Some girl, donkeys' years ago, had once told him after a college lecture that he resembled a Marathi film star whose name he had never heard. This was the closest Vaibhav Kulkarni had ever gotten to receiving a compliment. What nature could not grant him in the department of looks, it compensated by giving him a very large and pure heart. Only, the obvious benefits of possessing a pure heart were far and few. And only three people in the world really gave a damn about the purity of his heart – his daughter, and his now dead parents. Not that he craved any more, really.

'Mangal Pandey was the pioneer of the Indian Mutiny,' he prodded her. 'We read this last week, do you remember now?'

'Who was Raja Ram Mohan Roy?' she craned her head over his shoulder.

'The father of the Indian Renaissance,' he replied.

'That was close.'

'That is not something your history teacher would be happy to hear,' he said distractedly.

They halted at yet another traffic signal. The sixth one that morning, he silently counted to himself per habit. He looked at his watch and gulped nervously. He did not remember now who had once told him Pune was called a pensioner's paradise. The only paradise he had ever known was his old home in Akola, the quiet, distilled town he had left for good. Pune was bursting at its seams. In the four years since he had come here with Nisha, he had steadily seen a somewhat calm city transform into just another metropolis he found himself a misfit in. He never complained about this to anyone, for two prime reasons: one, it was his own calculated decision at some time in the past to shift base to Pune. And two, he had no one to complain to anyway. His daughter had fallen in love with

Pune. And his only friend in the city, Bhandari, would only hand him another of those self-help books providing inner peace if he even thought of complaining.

Akola had left little to add to Vaibhav's fortune, besides a bag of mixed memories. The land he had inherited was practically infertile. Then an attempted business partnership in a stagnant real estate market started showing signs of tanking before even taking off. Two important events followed: one, he realized that the concept of good karma was fiction; and two, he underwent a fast-track diploma course in network administration in lieu of the college degree he had left incomplete owing to his father's tireless faith in their ancestral land. The diploma may not have been an idea that changed his life. But it at least got him a regular job as a systems administrator in Pune after having made a pitch to every possible contact.

He looked at himself in the side-view mirror sadly. 'I look old now, don't I?'

'No you don't,' she said. 'Thirty-five is not old.'

'What is old, then?'

'Hmm, forty plus, maybe?'

'Still have five more years, eh?' He laughed. 'But look here. My sideburns are turning grey already.' He placed a finger near his ear.

'They look good,' she asserted. 'Even George Clooney has grey hair. But he is handsome. Papa, let's go.'

The signal turned green. On cue, an unpleasant symphony of car horns barked at his heels. He fumbled a little as he kicked the engine to a start. Every extra minute on the road seemed to exponentially add volume to the traffic.

'My history teacher likes me,' Nisha responded to their earlier unfinished conversation.

Vaibhav smiled. 'Everyone likes you. But that does not exempt you from knowing your history.'

'I have been wanting to tell you,' she spoke cautiously, 'that I do not enjoy studying History.'

'Why not?'

'I don't understand it,' she insisted. 'I was also wondering – had you not once told me we must always look to the future in order to be successful? Then why do we need to study something that happened in the past?'

'Because you cannot build a solid future without respecting and understanding your past.'

'I think I am much better at Geography,' she swiftly changed the subject.

His phone began ringing. 'One quick halt,' he said as he pulled over to a side.

'Papa, I am late,' she reminded him.

'I know, I know,' he hurriedly fetched his phone from his shirt pocket. He looked at the screen, shook his head, and resumed driving.

'Alright, so where were we? Yes, Geography,' he remembered. 'Ok. What passes through twenty-three degrees latit...'

'The Tropic of Cancer,' she replied before he could finish asking the question. Her eyes searched his face for a gesture of appreciation.

They took a slip road off the busy University road into the lane leading to her school.

'Which country is the largest producer of iron ore?' he asked.

'The People's Republic of China,' she replied just as promptly.

'What is the capital of Indonesia?'

'Bali...' she said, and her voice trailed off as soon as she heard her father burst into peals of laughter.

'I meant Jakarta and you know that,' she spoke with some aggression by her standards.

'Bali, Bali!' he chuckled as they pulled over some fifty feet away from the school gate.

It had been a routine for nearly four years now. But Nisha never asked her father why he never dropped her off right at the school gate. She probably never noticed it. Vaibhav had never noticed it himself. His subconscious state, however, never failed to note he was among the very few parents who did not drop their child off in the kind of car he could not even dream of buying.

'Papa please, stop,' she moaned, thumping her helmet in his lap.

'Alright, alright,' he relented. 'I will be off now. Do you need some money?'

'No, I am good.'

'Nisha!' a thin voice boomed from inside the school gates. They turned around to see a heavy-set boy of her age come running towards them.

'I think that is the capital of Indonesia coming to get you,' Vaibhav said with a straight face.

'Papa, please,' she frowned at him, and then turned to the boy whose ample cheeks now flushed a deep red. 'Hi, Bali.'

Bali flashed his toothy grin at Nisha and then turned to Vaibhav. 'Good morning, Uncle.'

'Oh, good morning, Bali,' said Vaibhav, pretending he had not noticed the boy. 'Sorry I did not recognize you from a distance. I have never seen you run like that before.' He revved his engine again. 'Ok, off with you two. I am running late...hey. What's that on your head?'

Nisha hurriedly pushed a few errant strands of her hair behind her ear. Vaibhav turned her head around and rolled his eyes in horror on seeing three strands coloured pink.

'Who did that to you?' he demanded.

'Papa!' Nisha gestured him to soften down. 'Sunaina took me to her salon yesterday after school...'

Bali giggled. 'I think it looks hot, yaar.'

'Aye!' Vaibhav looked at Bali irritably. 'Don't use that word. Young kids are not supposed to look hot. They are not supposed to go to salons. Nisha, we do not go to salons. There is an age and time for all this, and this is not it. Do you get it? And who is this Sunaina?'

'Sunaina Dalal from my class,' she reminded him, not for the first time.

Vaibhav cringed at her coloured hair strands. 'I don't think Rihanna would have coloured her hair when she was ten.'

Nisha, who idolized the pop star, knew Rihanna's Wikipedia page like the back of her hand. 'She does, now.'

'Very good,' said Vaibhav. 'Colour your hair when you are that age, then. Now run along, so I can run along too. And remember, straight to Leena Madam's after school. I will pick you up from her place at six.'

'Alright, bye.'

He watched over her until she disappeared into the crowd of children, with Bali tailing her closely like the loyal friend he had always been. Nisha's transformation from a quiet, reserved newcomer to being the school's hallmark student had taken the teachers and students by surprise. In the winter of 2010 when

Vaibhav had read a leaflet advertising a new privately funded school that boasted of an international curriculum, he had not imagined it would trigger a crucial twist in his life. He procured a print of the application form for the aptitude entrance test. Nisha scored an ace. Well-wishers convinced him there was a lot of merit in the idea of selling his ancestral property in Akola and moving his daughter to a bigger city for a better, wholesome education. He did not bother doing a cost benefit analysis on this decision, because when he had done so earlier, he had learnt that both the costs and the benefits of every decision were always momentary. He sold off his ancestral property as well as the memories of over thirty years, moved to Pune, and got Nisha admitted to arguably one of Maharashtra's most coveted schools, entirely on her merit. He then bought them a modest apartment in Pimple Saudagar which, much to his dismay did not get covered by what he made by selling off what he had in Akola. A small home loan was taken above all that he was in possession of. The loan had two adverse effects: one, he had to carefully balance the art of pinching pennies while ensuring that his daughter's dream of being the next Rihanna transformed into reality one day. And the second was this phone call that he had been getting almost every week for over a year. That morning, he had been getting this phone call with some sense of urgency. He finally scrambled to answer it as he parked his bike in the office garage.

'Rachna, I am so sorry I have been missing your calls,' he began. 'I was driving and have been very rushed.'

'Sir,' said his banking officer at the other end. 'Please. You do not need to be sorry.'

There was an obvious tone of surprise in her voice. All those years that she had peddled credit card offers to unsuspecting customers on the phone, all she had received was indifference, grumpiness, or abruptly disconnected conversations. She was not prepared to have a customer apologize to her for holding on. She knew Vaibhav was different, even if he had not entirely bought into her pitch.

'Sir, did you consider that offer of our new credit card?' she asked with renewed excitement. 'I wanted to tell you there are some new benefits that you can now avail of.'

He darted across the parking lot towards the office elevator. 'Aha. I have not made up my mind yet. But I promise to.'

'Sir, we can waive off fifty percent of your card purchase cost,' she offered. 'And you also stand to win a new Nokia Smartphone if you become an early bird subscriber.'

'Can you give me one more day?' he asked. 'I will have an answer for you by tomorrow evening. I promise.'

Rachna smiled victoriously. 'Of course, sir. Tomorrow evening it will be.'

He clicked his phone shut. Presently the door of the elevator opened. He stepped in to find the singular face that had played a pivotal role in spiking up his stress hormones in the last year or more.

'Hello, Vaibhav!' Samar Yadav greeted him with the most obviously fake smile anyone could sport. 'You are late.'

Yes, he was late indeed. Vaibhav noted this was not the first time he was late. He also noted this would not be the first time he would tell Samar that *he* was not the authority to tell him he was late to work – or for that matter, that Samar did not have *any* authority over Vaibhav at work or otherwise. And that if Samar were to put his glibness aside, he was not half as competent a brain as Vaibhav was. But Vaibhav chose to stay quiet that morning, for there was only so much bad blood that he could withstand at work as he had already created.

'Taneja was looking for you a while back,' Samar added when he got no response from Vaibhav. 'I was on my way down to pick up my coffee when I saw him hovering around your desk.'

'What was he saying?' Vaibhav asked nervously.

'He was a little crabby about the batch run that failed last night,' he replied.

'The batch run failed again?' Vaibhav asked. 'And why was he after me for it anyway? I am not officially assigned to the batch run.'

Samar grinned mischievously. 'It is the soy, Vaibhav. Taneja drinks too much soy. It makes him jumpy. And then he tends to lose his bearings. Don't worry, just go talk to him.'

Vaibhav went straight to Taneja's cabin with all the right questions and defences. But it turned out he still owed Taneja some sort of explanation as to why the batch job failed the previous night.

'As you know, it was not my turn to monitor the batch last night.' Vaibhav's voice trembled and choked every time he consciously tried to curb his anger. 'And we both know whose turn it actually was.'

Taneja had calmed down a bit by now. 'Sit down. Yes, we both also know that Samar is a nut. This is not the first time he has given us the slip. But we are a team, Vaibhav. And we've got to do what a team's got to do.'

'But I have already told you I can stay in late once a week. No more.' Vaibhav resented.

Taneja smiled. 'Do you think of me as the clichéd prick of a boss who lets his subordinates get snowed under work?'

'You know that is not how I think about you,' said Vaibhav. 'I appreciate that you bend the rules for me so often, despite my numerous constraints.'

Taneja picked up his whiteboard marker as a matter of habit to proffer a detailed explanation. Then he dropped the idea. Vaibhav heaved a sigh of relief.

'Vaibhav Kulkarni, systems administrator with Synergy,' he pronounced the designation in a high pitch. 'Do you remember the first thing I had told you when you had joined us three years ago?'

'Yes. That this world is full of cruel people.'

Taneja burst out laughing. 'You witty, witty man. Sharp sense of humour. Ok, what was the second thing I had said?'

'Don't believe everything people tell you.'

Taneja sighed. 'Let me remind you.' He gestured a forward jump and rolled his eyes hopefully. 'Yes?'

'Take a forward leap.'

'Bravo!' Taneja exclaimed victoriously. 'And that is what I have liked about you. I like your attitude of going beyond your designated role and understanding other functions in the organization. You have been a keen learner. All I am asking of you is that you put your additional knowledge to use and help that Samar donkey do his work better.'

'I have spent more time here performing other roles than my own,' he reminded Taneja. 'But on Pay Day, I am still only a systems administrator.'

Taneja drew an imaginary circle with his finger. 'It is a matter of time, buddy. Circle of life. You won't go unrewarded.'

Vaibhav sensed they were arriving at a dead end. 'What can I do to help?'

'Fix the damned batch job please,' Taneja sighed. 'Stay in late today if you must. Do it alone if you must. But please handle it.'

'I will,' Vaibhav said, although somewhat reluctantly, and got up to leave.

'Vaibhav.' Taneja called after him.

'Yes?'

Taneja smiled. 'How is Nisha doing?'

A broad smile flashed across Vaibhav's face. 'Wonderful, as always.'

'I can see she is going to grow up to be far brighter than her father,' Taneja winked. 'What do you think?'

'No debates there!' He grinned heartily.

He went to his seat and got down to work. Fixing the batch job had appeared to be a giant task, but he fixed it within hours. When he had got it out of the way, he realized it was well past lunch time. He opted to skip the long walk to the canteen and spread out his tiffin at his desk instead. His cubicle was at the quietest corner of the floor. The window by his side afforded him a partial view of The Royal Pune Club. The chatter of members' children wallowing around in the swimming pool had started on schedule. He looked at the time: it was nearing four in the evening. He spooned some okra from his tiffin with a piece of chapatti. A puddle of oil dripped from his fist and settled on the tiffin cover. He cleared it sincerely with a finger and looked out of the window again. The reflection of the water from the pool formed a wavy pattern on his window frame. Children inside the pool squealed with delight once again. Their voices resonated through the still air. He lapped up the remaining morsels of his lunch before turning his attention back to the emails that still needed his attention before he could call it a day.

Now they say that dreams are just for fools

He stands at the edge of the dark blue pool. Swim lanes have been demarcated by thick ropes along the length of the pool. He can feel the chill of the water even as he stands outside it. He is flanked by boys his age on either side, ready to plunge. Casio watches adorn some wrists. He had only vaguely heard of the brand thus far. He is looking at it closely for the first time. The audience lets out an applause, which brings his attention back to the job at hand. Overhead, he sees a large banner of cloth that reads "Annual Maharashtra Sports Festival, 1993 – Welcome to Mumbai". The tension soars. He looks towards the stands so he can spot his mother waving at him. But all he sees is a blur. Then he hears the gunshot fire.

He dives. His heart throbs violently as his nimble limbs help him gain over his competitors. He can feel their silhouettes inside the water, next to him. But he keeps his focus and his energy. He splashes faster. He does not care to breathe, not until his little fingers feel the wall at the *other end of the pool. He leaps out of the pool to a deafening applause.*

'For the second time in a row, Vaibhav Kulkarni from Akola Public School retains the title of the Maharashtra swimming champion in the under-14 category...'

'Are you tired?'

He felt Nisha's tiny palm tap his tired shoulders. Vaibhav woke up from his desk, dazed and hungry.

'Power nap,' he replied, shutting down the medieval-era computer he had been trying to sell off. 'Are you ready for dinner?'

'Yes, I have finished my home assignments,' she said, reaching out for the television placed in their bonsai living room.

She tuned in to *Indian Idol* and joined Vaibhav in the kitchen to help him warm the food and to lay out the plates. Intermittently, they shared their respective opinions about the performances of the participants. Vaibhav tried sounding as confident as he could while talking music, but he could not fool anyone. He was a clear nut when it came to understanding music. But he rarely missed asking Nisha to sing him something before they both retired to bed. And then he would tell her how she could have sung that line a little softer, or punctuated that stanza with a higher note. Nisha never told him she knew better. She never even told him that Leena Madam, her music teacher, had once joked that Vaibhav looked "very cute" when he tried talking music.

Now weeks ahead of her inter-class singing competition, Vaibhav sat longer hours after dinner to help with her rehearsals. They took to their couch – a second-hand, rusted sofa which was among the very sparse furnishings in their living room. Others included a round dining table for three. One of those three chairs mostly stayed unoccupied. The walls of the house had cement peeling off various seeping crevices. There were few photographs or trinkets available to hide the seepage. So they tried seeing the positives of possessing seeping walls, although they could never see any.

'Ask Leena Madam to review your rehearsals,' he suggested before returning to his room for the night. 'You are good, but you can be better.'

Nisha returned to her room and lay in bed with the lights off, pretending to be asleep. But she didn't blink until she had finished her mandatory nightly routine of imagining herself warding off overenthusiastic crowds from thronging her at her maiden concert. Twenty minutes later, she was put to sleep by Vaibhav's enormously loud but systematic snores from the adjacent room, which often doubled up as a lullaby.

The next morning Vaibhav woke up earlier than usual. His weeklong preoccupation with the 'Clean Up Samar Yadav's Coding Errors' assignment had finally ended. At the end of which, by the way, Taneja had congratulated him and complimented him for being a "team player". Ten minutes after that, he had heard Taneja walk past Samar's cubicle and call him a team player too. But the good news was that the Vaibhav Kulkarni Charity had shut shop until further notice. This gave him time to fix up a lunch appointment with Bhandari – his only friend existent on the face of the earth. The maid had prepared potatoes and rotis early in the morning, which were duly refrigerated for consumption at dinner. He rode Nisha to school, handed her a hundred so she could buy lunch from the cafeteria – *do not compromise on quality* – he reminded her at least thrice, almost guilty both of shelling out a hundred and of the fear that a hundred might not potentially suffice for a hearty meal at *Goodwill International School*. Nisha convinced him a fifty would have been more than enough.

'Just in case,' he insisted and rode away.

He approached The Royal Pune Club with the same nervousness he had felt when he had set foot outside the Pune railway station for the first time four years ago. The nervousness of a misfit and of the likelihood of getting it all wrong. The wrought iron gates of the club had rusted from the rains. But to him they were only a pair of overbearing, enormous beasts that made him reconsider his desire to pass through them. He slowed his bike as he approached the security guard, presuming he was going to be questioned about his business on these exotic premises. But the guard just half-stood up from his chair, examined Vaibhav with little interest, and half-saluted him with a half-smile.

'Visitors' parking?' Vaibhav asked uncertainly. The guard motioned through the gates towards a line of cars glistening in all their unaffordable splendour in the open parking bay. Vaibhav drove into the parking lot and parked his bike as far as possible from the fancy machines – if for some godforsaken reason a molecule of his motorcycle were to rub against the polished richness of metals, the compensation could be worth more than the purchase price of the motorcycle itself.

The club was aptly named. Largely retained in its original form, it bore a huge colonial flavour in terms of its structure and grandeur. The landscaping was lavish and immaculate. The roads looked nurtured by layers of Cherry Blossom or whatever. He watched people stream into and out of the reception area. Club members were dressed in clothes that looked elegant even when soaked in litres of sweat. Everything about this place was perfect, too perfect for him to stand up to and ask the single question he was here for. Beyond the reception area, he saw the alluring blue water from the pool. At the reception desk sat a middle-aged man who had Achilles-dived headfirst into a lake of hair gel. The hair on his head were far and few, but whatever existed stood on the scalp in perfect posture. An elderly gentleman and his wife stood next to him, engaged in small talk. Hair Gel laughed politely on schedule, in response to everything the couple said. As Vaibhav approached them, the intensity of his laughter reduced. He continued nodding at the couple, with half a gaze fixed curiously on Vaibhav. The kind of gaze that makes you feel like a suspect. Vaibhav slinked away and went straight towards the swimming pool. It was close to nine in the morning and the crowd had thinned considerably. Three very evidently retired men lazed around in the blue water, speaking again in the kind of English that Vaibhav understood but did not speak. With every splash they made, a chunk of memories from his yesteryears came floating toward him. When he could take no more, he returned to the reception.

The crowd at the reception had increased. Hair Gel had gotten busier in being polite and in concealing his boredom. The question was on the tip of Vaibhav's tongue. It needed to be asked *now*. But it did not get asked. Hair Gel did not look happy enough for a first conversation. Maybe there was a Samar Yadav in every profession, Vaibhav gathered. *Some other day, soon.*

He returned to the parking lot and was walking towards his bike when a sixty-something golfer in a Ralph Lauren shirt intercepted him and made enquiries about the weather and other things that had never crossed his busy mind all these years. Vaibhav said it was wonderful to meet him too and the weather was fantastic and if only he were on a long drive to a much-needed vacation resort, it would have felt even better. Deep into the conversation the golfer realized they had not met before and some introductions were overdue, so he asked of Vaibhav's name and why he had not spotted him at the club more often earlier. Vaibhav gave out his name, withholding other details, and explained that he had been overseas, working in London for years and had only just come back recently because he had been feeling utterly patriotic. Discreetly wiping sweat off his brow, he secretly prayed this conversation would end soon. But in a cruel twist of fate, the golfer had lived in London nearly eight years and his excitement had now doubled – where did Vaibhav stay, in the city or in the suburbs? How far from Canary Wharf where the golfer's former penthouse apartment was? Had Vaibhav met the Queen whilst he was there?

That last question had not been asked yet, but Vaibhav feared they were not too far from it. So he started excusing himself politely, saying he was running late for work, which he now realized he indeed was.

'Let me walk you to your car,' the golfer suggested.

Yes, exactly the kind of situation Vaibhav needed to realize that you are likely to run into friendly people only at all the wrong times. He quietly slid the key of his bike into the pocket of his trousers and led the golfer towards nowhere in particular before exclaiming, 'Ah, looks like my driver has not returned with the car yet.'

The golfer would hear no word of resentment as he insisted on dropping Vaibhav to his office.

'Come on, you told me it is barely a mile from here,' said the golfer. 'Let me drop you. Call your driver and ask him to report straight at your office.'

Tired, Vaibhav accepted the car ride and put up with another five minutes of pretending to be God's gift to the Indian economy. The golfer's Audi was a little bigger than Vaibhav's bedroom, or so he thought as he examined it enviously. Far from having sat in one, this was the first time Vaibhav had *touched* or *breathed near* an Audi. He felt grand, but also very worried about having left his bike behind in the club. But then, the bike could wait. No one in *that* club would bother doing things to his bike. He got dropped off at his office gates, duly thanked the golfer, silently prayed he would never run into him again, and darted straight into the office to make up for lost time.

Because no unforeseen crisis had occurred in the company that morning, no one had noticed his absence. He silently took his seat in his working bay, knocked off his routine emails, and stayed put just in case people noticed he had stayed off work for uncharacteristically long that day. Shortly before his appointed lunch with Bhandari, he walked the long sunny walk back to the club to pick up his bike. To his horror, the bike was missing from where he had left it. On making enquiries with the receptionist (a happier man had replaced Hair Gel in the shift), he learnt that the bike's registration number was not included in the club's roster, which is why Hair Gel had reported it as a suspicious item that had made its way into the club premises. When no one turned up to claim the "item" in more than an hour, Hair Gel had called the police and had got it transported to the nearest police station.

By now, of course, Vaibhav had lost all appetite for lunch. He telephoned Bhandari and asked him to come over to the

Camp Police Station; that he would give details later. He then sprinted out of the club and hailed an autorickshaw zipping along the other end of the road. The auto driver saw the outstretched hand, manoeuvred a U-turn without reducing his speed, and nearly landed on Vaibhav's toe.

'Camp police station?' Vaibhav asked as he settled inside the rickshaw without waiting for approval.

The rickshaw driver massaged his gums thoughtfully, and asked, 'Where about the Camp police station?'

'How many of them are there?' Vaibhav asked irritably. 'Just one. Take me there.'

As though calibrating a meter in his head, the auto driver frowned. 'Hmm. Sixty rupees.'

'Boss! It is just two min...well, ok.' He was too tired to haggle.

The happy auto driver deposited Vaibhav outside the police station in less than two minutes, charged him sixty rupees and drove away merrily. Vaibhav entered the office to find Bhandari waiting for him as promised. Nearly his age and descent, Bhandari was a 1.1 version of Vaibhav Kulkarni. He was clean shaven, his body was under constant maintenance at an annual membership charge levied by Gold's Gym, and he wore an expensive Burberry perfume which Vaibhav for the longest time had been mistakenly hearing as "Blackberry". When they were both together, though, it was hard to imagine it had been over twenty-one years since they last shared that rickety wooden bench in Akola Public High School.

'What have you done?' Bhandari stood up to greet him.

'A long story,' Vaibhav replied as he continued walking towards the police inspector in charge.

'Sir, my bike has been brought here,' began Vaibhav. 'I am here to collect it.'

'Why was it brought here?' demanded the cop without looking up from the register he was poring into.

'I do not know, sir,' replied Vaibhav.

'Then you must find out first, no?' the cop asked, still refusing to lift his gaze.

'We are sorry, sir,' Bhandari decided to intervene. 'We are sorry for whatever it was picked up for. If we could please collect it...'

'Registration number?'

The cop looked up at Vaibhav for the first time when he heard the registration number.

'What business did you have leaving your vehicle at the club?' the cop demanded angrily.

Indeed. He had no business leaving the vehicle at the club. He had no business being at the club in the first place. And now he owed an explanation not only to one angry policeman, but also to a very curious Bhandari who had a lot of business understanding what had urged him to go to The Royal Pune Club out of the blue. The formalities took under ten minutes, during which time Vaibhav tried substituting a penalty of three hundred rupees with around thirty utterances of an apology. But the cop would hear none of it and those three hundred rupees and some invisible tears were shelled out.

When they stepped out on the road, Bhandari looked at Vaibhav with the expected curiosity.

'Sorry to be a prick,' Vaibhav said, his face hung low from the penalty. 'Can we do lunch some other day?'

Bhandari considered him for some time before replying. 'Shut up. And let's go.'

They settled at The Blue Nile after some argument. A basic Iranian diner with extraordinary food. Bhandari brandished two lunch vouchers before Vaibhav and declared the lunch was free. Of course, he brandished them fast enough for Vaibhav to not realize that those were actually vouchers for drinks at Out Of The Blue, and that Bhandari would quietly foot the bill at the reception after lunch under the pretext of taking a leak.

'Would you care to explain?' the question was asked again.

And thus, Vaibhav gave an account of the entire event over *roomali rotis* and butter chicken. The view of the swimming pool had been poking him for far too long and he had gone to the club with a half-mind to bring closure to this feeling of unrest. At the club he got cold feet and had nearly forgotten what he had gone there for. Then those sneering looks from Hair Gel made him feel like Sudama had lost his way into the kingdom of Dwarka or something. And then he lost his senses somewhere in the fragrant leather of the golfer's Audi and left the bike unattended and that he should never have given a thought to the swimming pool in the first place and that he should have known better about middle-class constraints and his home loan and his daughter's educational loan.

Bhandari, who had acquired an honours' degree in Get Vaibhav A Life, was now devouring his chicken with angry swallows. Not for the first time that day did he remind his old friend that there were little joys beyond parenting and worrying about the future.

'That father inside you is not going to drown if you get inside that goddamn pool,' he said.

'The goddamn pool is goddamn-er expensive,' Vaibhav observed sadly.

'You figured out by smelling the water?' asked Bhandari. 'Or did you check?'

'I did not check,' came the reply. 'I chickened out. I just told you.'

Bhandari picked up a handful of tissues and wiped his greasy fingers urgently. 'Let us check now.'

He pulled out his iPhone and searched membership fees at The Royal Pune Club Online. Two minutes later he had a look of horror on his face. Three minutes later he returned an embarrassed look to Vaibhav.

'Alright, so it *is* goddamn-er expensive,' Bhandari conceded. 'But listen. Go talk to them anyway. Tell them you don't want to pluck diamond chunks off the walls of the club. You only need to use the pool. They will work something out.'

'You think so?'

'I know so. Just do it.'

That was settled, then. Vaibhav would freshly file an application for Some Courage. Upon its acquisition he would visit the club again and try not making a fool of himself. Bhandari then went to "use the vouchers" on his way to the bathroom before the two friends went about their diverse schedules for the rest of the day.

On returning to his working bay, Vaibhav discovered he had been missed. Taneja had left eighteen calls on his desk phone, which was frustrating if not abnormal. Vaibhav made a visit to the big man's cabin and learnt that there was a proposal for a prospective Brazilian client that needed to be worked on. 'Of course it does not fall under the ambit of your role,' Taneja began to explain.

'But I am a team player?' Vaibhav offered to complete the explanation for him.

'Yes! You are one, aren't you? Listen,' continued Taneja, 'if we can crack this deal, I want you to take centrestage on this project. Understand?'

And hence it was decided that Vaibhav would work with Samar Yadav on this very crucial proposal, which basically meant Vaibhav would work alone on this very crucial proposal. He had a quick look at the requirement. It was an assignment he had never done before, but which involved a technology that he had come to understand with time. He visited Taneja again later that afternoon and told him he wanted to go solo on this proposal and that he did not want to involve Samar.

'Makes absolute sense to me,' said Taneja. 'I am myself a little fed up of that man. Just involve him in advisory matters if you need to.'

Vaibhav considered reminding him that Samar was not senior or smart enough to advise him on any matter whatsoever. But the last time he had tried explaining how Samar tried overriding anything he said or did, Taneja had put him through a four-hour long intensive online tutorial on Assertiveness Skills while Samar had the last laugh. This time, Vaibhav chose to keep quiet. He made some progress on the task at hand during the rest of the day. As he was leaving, he received an email from Samar (marking Taneja) asking for an update on the progress.

Fuming, he stormed out of the office without bothering to reply. He drove straight to Leena Madam's, where Nisha waited for him as always.

'How was your day?' she asked the conventional question as she sat pillion on the motorcycle.

'Wonderful, as always,' came the even more conventional reply.

It's just a little crush

'Congratulations sir, you are now a minute away from holding your credit card in your hands!'

Rachna waved a card before Vaibhav's dreamy eyes.

Vaibhav cleared his throat. 'A credit limit of fifty thousand, did you say?'

'Yes, which we will increase next year,' she was almost screaming with excitement now. 'And as promised, sir, here is your phone.'

She handed him a Nokia phone the features of which he did not care to understand even as she rattled them off the tip of her tongue. She also gave him a long list of dos and don'ts in regard with use of the credit card, also which he paid little attention to. His happiness knew no bounds. He needed to speak to Nisha right away. He called Bali on his cell phone – nearly every student of the school owned a cell phone, except his daughter (until then) – and demanded to speak to Nisha.

'Uncle, she is at the song rehearsals,' Bali informed him. 'She is up next on stage. Can I make her call you back?'

'Don't tell me you are singing too,' Vaibhav teased him.

'I am the audience,' Bali said shyly. He sang terribly alright, but not as terribly as the person at the other end of the conversation.

'Can you give her the phone for just a second?' Vaibhav asked again. 'I am sure you are in the auditorium right now?'

'I am,' said Bali. 'But she is on stage already. And the teachers have given all of them only three minutes each with the orchestra.'

'You know what, just tell her I have a surprise for her,' Vaibhav said, barely able to conceal his excitement. 'Tell her I will pick her up from school at four.'

Just then, the silence in the auditorium was ruptured by Nisha's voice as the orchestra joined in. Vaibhav stayed on the line for a minute so he could listen to her sing. When he saw Samar make animated gestures about some proposal-related update he was unnecessarily waiting for, he clicked the phone shut and reluctantly returned to his desk. Meanwhile Nisha continued creating ripples in the auditorium for the next three minutes. She was the school's model student in every sense of the word – a favourite of teachers and students alike. The teachers liked her because she was a top grader. The students liked her even more because she never thought twice before lending a helping hand to the lower graders who always got her handwritten notes photocopied ahead of their exams. But in front of the microphone, Nisha's stardom went up a notch.

As Miss Suzanne, the school's English teacher, said, 'Nisha is meant for something very big. Little Indian Idol, maybe?' And then she looked at the other students who had been idling away in that auditorium as spectators only so they would not have to be in their classrooms: 'Children, having fun does not mean not being responsible towards your future. You ought to learn something from Nisha.'

Miss Suzanne strode up to Nisha and reiterated her faith in the girl's talent. 'Keep it up, darling. You know you are going to win the competition.'

'I will try my best, ma'am, thank you,' Nisha smiled politely. *Don't let them get to your head*, she thought of what her father told her about people's compliments. (Not that he had much experience with compliments, but yes, he did know a thing or two about modesty).

'I hope your father is coming to watch you perform,' asked Miss Suzanne.

'He has promised to,' Nisha said. 'He will leave work early that day so he can get here in time.'

'He had better,' she spoke in mock anger. 'And tell him I have a bone to pick with him, so he must see me when he is here.'

'What happened, ma'am?' asked Nisha, worried.

'I have been telling him to bring you over for a meal to my house,' she said. 'And he keeps avoiding the discussion. Tell him I am not a half bad cook, will you?'

Bali suppressed a snigger, which drew a sharp gaze from Miss Suzanne. 'Something's funny and I don't see it, huh, Bali?'

'No ma'am, I am sorry,' Bali said, looking the other way.

'I will tell him to speak to you, ma'am,' assured Nisha. 'We will surely come over soon.'

Miss Suzanne pulled her cheeks until they turned ruddy red, then offered another stern gaze to Bali, and walked away.

'What were you laughing for?' Nisha turned to Bali as they started walking out of the auditorium.

'You won't believe me if I told you,' Bali quipped as though he were going to quote something straight out of Wikipedia.

'Try me,' she said, her attention now wholly towards him.

'Miss Suzanne has the hots for your dad,' he giggled. 'Don't tell me you don't know it.'

'What rubbish, Bali. Shut up!'

'No, I am serious,' he insisted. 'I can see it in her eyes. I was watching her at the annual day last year when she was speaking to him. You just know she wants him!'

Nisha thwacked Bali on the shoulder. 'Shut up! Don't dare say a word more about Papa.'

'No, no, I am not saying anything about Uncle,' he clarified. 'I am talking about her. I know Uncle has never looked at Miss Suzanne upward of her tired stilettos.'

'Alright Bali, enough,' she said. 'Tell me what did I miss in the Algebra class when I left for practice?'

'The world came crashing down,' he smiled, and then added, 'Nothing. Relax. Just a home assignment.'

'What home assignment?'

'Choose fifteen sums on complex and simple interest from the textbook and solve them on your own,' he mimicked the tone of their Algebra teacher.

He then pulled out a new notebook from his satchel and handed it to Nisha. 'Here, I have done eight for you. Complete the rest on your own.'

She opened the notebook with surprise to see eight sums *correctly* solved in Bali's obnoxious handwriting. She smiled and thanked him, but he brushed it off by reminding her that she had helped him the previous year with those crappy Botany lessons two days ahead of their exams, and they were now square.

'Eight sums against helping you prepare for an entire exam?' Nisha teased him. 'That is not exactly being square.'

'That is all I can do,' he yawned, stretching his ample torso lazily. 'Other than filling you in on who has been hitting on your father lately.'

He laughed and ran as she followed him to smack him on the shoulder again. Needless to say, he could not run for too long. All the "organic chips" he had been snacking on lately were catching up. He duly received another slap on the shoulder before remembering that Vaibhav had left a message for her.

'It is ten minutes past four, duffer!' Nisha exclaimed, looking at her watch.

'Let us run,' he took a lead on her, prodding her as he ran past her. 'Don't worry. Uncle will still be at the gate when we get there. Unless, of course, our fair lady Miss Suzanne has caught up with him before us!'

'You have had it!' Nisha chased Bali to the gate.

They huffed and puffed their way to the gate with their satchels strapped across their shoulders. Vaibhav waved at Nisha and reached out for the satchel. Slinging it over the handle of the motorcycle, he asked the children why they had been running.

'Bali forgot to tell me you were waiting for me,' Nisha told him. She stood behind Vaibhav and suppressed a smirk on seeing Bali's shocked expression.

'Nothing unexpected there,' Vaibhav shook his head. 'Bali, you need to eat more almonds.'

'Uncle, I had not forgotten,' Bali explained weakly. 'I was just getting around to telling her, but then we got into an important discussion.'

'Tell Papa about it,' Nisha cajoled him, laughing. 'Papa, Bali has made an observation he wants to tell you about.'

Bali went white with fear. 'Rubbish! No Uncle, it's nothing.'

Vaibhav cocked a brow at both of them, demanding an explanation. Just then, a black Audi pulled over right behind them. Bali heaved a sigh of relief at the possible distraction. The rear door of the car opened and out of it emerged Bali's mother, a thirty-something elegant, well bred and well kept woman. She wore a crisp white shirt, beige trousers (Vero Moda, Nisha noted), and a pair of sunglasses that now rested on her shampooed hair. It was nearing four-thirty in the evening, but she looked and smelt as fresh as a bad conductor to the dirt and grime of the city. Vaibhav took a quick look at his own shirt subconsciously – it was the "before" part of a Tide detergent advertisement. *Where does this woman work, in a South Pole igloo?*

'Hello, Mr. Kulkarni,' she strode forward with a smile and greeted him with an extended hand.

Handshakes were never an integral part of Vaibhav's educational and value system during childhood and boyhood. The locality he grew up in had theorized that a handshake between a boy and a girl only meant they were about to get naughty. And because being naughty was not a done thing in the locality, boys and girls never shook hands. When he moved to Pune, he underwent a weeklong induction on body language, corporate etiquette and yes, handshakes, at Synergy Software. It was here he discovered that handshakes were harmless and of three types: the firm handshake which indicated assertiveness, the sloppy handshake that indicated submissiveness, and the third kind that he invented – the "graze their fingers" handshake – which indicated unwillingness.

So when Bali's mother offered her hand, Vaibhav grazed her fingers with his as though he were measuring their temperature, and then instantly withdrew his palm and deposited it back in his pocket.

'Hello Mr. Khurana,' he said, and then stuck out his tongue in embarrassment. 'Sorry, Mrs.'

Mrs. Khurana pretended not to have heard the gaffe, and then turned to Nisha and lovingly asked her how she had been since the time they last met. Appropriate conversation followed. Mrs. Khurana then asked her if Bali had gotten any worthier as a student since the time he had carelessly studied for a Hindi exam a day before their Geography exam. Nisha was very generous in praising Bali and went overboard by telling her how he had solved eight sums for her that day while she was away rehearsing a song.

'Well, so we are participating in charity, Bali?' Mrs. Khurana scowled at her son. 'That is very nice, but only if we ever manage to complete our own homework in time, right?'

Some more words were exchanged between the mother and her son, which ended with her saying, 'We need to talk.'

Deathly silence followed, after which Mrs. Khurana turned to Vaibhav again. 'I am so glad I found you here, Mr. Kulkarni. I was thinking of calling you anyway.'

'Yes, please?' Vaibhav asked, puzzled.

'There has been a lot of buzz and excitement about Nisha's birthday next month amongst these kids,' Mrs. Khurana began. 'And I think that is fairly obvious given how popular your little girl is in her class!'

Nisha smiled graciously as she had always been taught to on being offered a generous compliment.

'And, Mr. Kulkarni, the kids still keep raving about how much fun they had at her last birthday at your apartment,' she continued, and then her voice trailed off a little. 'This year, though, they have been keen to plan something grander. You know how these kids are, don't you?'

Vaibhav wondered where this was going. Wherever it was going, however, it needed to go fast. There was only so long that he could meet the woman's fixed, confident gaze in conversation. He also observed the use of "grander" in comparative. That was not a point worth contesting. A birthday party at his modest apartment did not accommodate grandeur. She could have just used "grand" and she would have still been right. Bali nudged his mother in a bid to hurry her up.

'Our friends have a farmhouse in Nigdi that lies vacant most of the year,' she continued. 'It just occurred to me the other day – and it is of course entirely up to you – but why don't we let the kids throw a big bash for Nisha at the farmhouse this year? It will be a lot more fun.'

Nisha's eyes lit up in anticipation. The delight in her expression was not lost on him, but Vaibhav pretended he had noticed nothing. *A lot more fun, indeed.*

'Thank you very much, Mrs. Khurana. But why must you bother? I will plan something closer to her birthday.' He was as assertive as he could allow himself to be. The reins of his daughter's Happiness And Welfare Management were not transferrable, even if the committee was housed in a two-bedroom apartment of *Savant Co-Operative Housing Society* aged twenty-eight years.

Mrs. Khurana had not sensed his discomfort at her suggestion of usurping control over his daughter's birthday celebrations. 'Oh come on, it is no botheration at all. Nisha is no less than our child too. And I don't even need to mention there are no costs attached to the venue. The owners are overseas and have left the property in our custody. It is all on the house!

The kids can call in pizzas and will have plenty of room to simply have a ball!'

Vaibhav stroked Nisha's hair. 'She is very lucky to have such thoughtful friends.' The sarcasm in his tone was well concealed under his respectful bow as he spoke. 'Thank you very much. I will surely give it a thought and let you know soon.'

Mrs. Khurana studied Vaibhav for a moment and then smiled in acceptance. Vaibhav studied her in return. There was no malice in her intent. She meant well. But she knew little about the pride of the middle-class Indian man. And that was not her fault. He grazed her fingers in that jittery Kulkarni handshake once again and said goodbye to both mother and son.

'After you,' he insisted, stretching his hand in the direction of their car. The last thing he wanted now was for her to notice how his motorcycle needed urgent servicing and oiling and then to offer her chauffer-driven car drive them to the Nigdi farmhouse. Once the dust kicked up by the speeding Audi had settled, he kicked his motorcycle to a start and patiently waited for Nisha to settle down on the seat.

It took him ten minutes to construct the question in his head before it finally came out. 'Nisha, did you want this party to be organized at the farmhouse?'

She chose her words carefully in order that they revealed nothing about what she wanted. 'It was not my idea.'

Hey, we're going to eat pizza!

After a brief debate between Pizza Hut and Subway, they chose the former. The closest Pizza Hut outlet was twenty minutes away from home on a nice evening, hence Vaibhav had budgeted their time accordingly.

'I know I want pasta in pesto sauce,' Nisha said, without looking at the menu.

'How do you know?' he asked her.

'I have been here before,' she said, 'for birthday lunches.'

'Why don't you try something different, then?' he suggested. 'There are so many pizzas; I feel full on reading the menu already.'

'Nothing beats this pasta,' she beamed. Dining out with her father was a rarity. The last time this had occurred was when he had got his last promotion. That was two years ago. This had to be a special day. She would ask him for details when he had finished scanning the six-page menu card.

'I cannot make up my mind,' he finally gave up and flipped the menu card on the table. 'Why don't you order a small pizza for me?'

He discreetly took out the food coupons that had come along with that beauty of a credit card. He read the fine lines. The food was being amply covered by two vouchers from the booklet. All was good. The steward arrived to take orders.

'May I have a bowl of pasta in pesto sauce and a chicken delight pan pizza, please?' Her diction and tone were moulded by fine education.

'Why don't we have a pitcher of masala lemonade too?' Vaibhav added.

'A pitcher of lemonade?' the steward confirmed and scribbled the order on his notepad. 'Done, sir.'

'You look very happy, Papa!' Nisha noted happily once the steward left the table.

'I am,' Vaibhav replied. 'I am happy with you because you have been a good girl all this year. And I must give you something for it.'

'What?'

'But you must promise me this will not spoil you,' he added as a note of caution. 'You need to keep your discipline in place.'

'Yes, Papa.'

He fetched the carefully wrapped phone from his office bag and handed it to her. She jumped out of her seat on seeing the contents of the packaging, and thanked her father excitedly.

'It is a smartphone,' he stated proudly as she flipped the pages of the user manual. 'You can download a lot of useful apps on it – but stick to the useful ones only. Save the games for until your summer vacation starts.'

'Ok,' she nodded. 'But why didn't you get it for yourself? Your phone is quite old too.'

'It suits my age,' he laughed at his own joke. 'And I hate these fancy phones anyway. They got no use for me.'

She smiled at him; there was a twinkle in her eyes. She might have been ten, but she was not the least bit ignorant of the many little sacrifices he had been making for her all along. The phone had to be among the more insignificant ones.

'I will use it only to make calls,' she assured him. 'And mostly only to you.'

'Very good,' he said. 'Now let us eat.'

The pizza and pasta had arrived and had brought with them a very inviting fragrance. Nisha dived straight into her bowl and began consuming the pasta by twirling her fork inside the bowl with practised ease. Vaibhav spent some time only admiring the crust of the pizza and accumulating all the molten cheese off its crust with his fingers.

'Ah, cheese is so much better when hot!' he smacked his finger happily.

He poured them both a glass each of the masala lemonade before returning to fondle the cheese.

'Papa, what do you think of Miss Suzanne?' Nisha asked suddenly.

The first bite of the sizzling crust had just made its way into Vaibhav's mouth. He struggled to send the morsel down his throat even as he stared at Nisha, confused.

'What do you mean?' he asked.

She giggled to dilute the intensity of the question. 'Ah, Bali and I think Miss Suzanne likes you.'

Vaibhav's cheeks instantly acquired the shade of the chilli flakes he was showering on his pizza slice. 'What? Of course not! Bali is mad! I don't want you to go mad too.'

'I love seeing you blush,' she laughed, wiping trails of sauce from the corners of her mouth.

Vaibhav shook his head and resumed eating. Even if Miss Suzanne did have a thing for him, and even in the remote chance he were to be tickled by such a prospect, he was too consumed by the taste and aroma of his food to bother about anything else. Pizzas were such a welcome change from the maid's indifferent cooking.

Nisha had now finished her dinner and was sipping on her lemonade, lost in thought. She had stopped smiling and was considering her father's mood. Cautiously, she approached him again. 'Papa, can I ask you something?'

'Sure.' He felt a sense of purpose in her tone and looked up.

'What happened to Mummy?'

In a parallel universe inside of Vaibhav, a storm broke out the moment the question was asked. Windows rattled. Glass panes shattered. The walls of Vaibhav's heart crumpled like a piece of sodden paper lying in the rain. Outside of him, the universe stayed unmoved. More customers had poured in and more pizzas were being served. The stewards were offering happy smiles to Vaibhav each time they passed by their table. Nisha sat stoically before him, waiting eagerly for an answer.

'Why do you ask?' was Vaibhav's first question. This was a good counter question. He had bought himself some time to come up with a response that would not sound ridiculous.

'Just like that,' came Nisha's frank reply. Uncomfortable questions did not need to be asked with a reason. They could always be asked just like that.

The leftover pizza on Vaibhav's plate had now self-transformed into an inedible, detestable rock of cold cheese and dough. He signalled to the steward to take it away from his sight before he showered it with a bout of vomit.

'I see,' he continued slowly after a long minute's pause. 'But why? We have talked about it before.'

'I don't remember anything, but,' she said, and then quickly added, 'Papa, are you mad at me for having asked this question?'

He may not have been mad at her. But he was obviously uneasy about it. He was miserable, in fact. The question had spoiled his party. But the innocence with which a little girl asks you that question can never be objected to. A question as plain and innocent as that has to be answered. He decided to use the technique his company HR always deployed when he asked them about salary hikes and promotions – The Synergy Software Proprietary of Lame Responses.

'Nisha, certain events in our lives are only driven by luck and circumstances,' he began. 'This is one of them. Your mother's destiny was not aligned with ours. That is all there is to it.'

If she felt dismay on hearing the response, Nisha did not show it. She tinkered with her phone instead, nodding silently, every movement of her curious eyes taking a generous stab at Vaibhav's heart.

'But hey,' Vaibhav brought her attention back to him. 'That does not mean she loves you any lesser than I do. Is that clear?'

'Yes,' Nisha forced a smile.

He watched her astutely as she took her time to finish eating.

'Do you want to leave?' he asked her. She nodded.

'Without taking a picture?' he asked her again.

'A picture?' She thought for a moment, and then said, 'Oh yes. Let us take a picture.'

The steward stepped forward graciously with his hands outstretched in search of a camera.

'Nisha, give him your smartphone, no?' Vaibhav spoke two decibels louder than he usually did.

'Phone,' Nisha corrected him softly, and handed the handset to the steward.

'Let the plastic be, please,' Vaibhav instructed him as Nisha took her position on the armrest of her father's chair.

The steward asked them to smile. Nisha smiled broadly. Vaibhav was still reeling from the question he had been asked, hence he so masked his sadness it looked like that smile was the biggest favour that had been bestowed upon the universe.

Nisha showed Vaibhav the maiden picture taken from the phone. 'It is very nice. Can we get it framed?'

'We must,' he said as he led her out towards their parked motorcycle.

This would be the second framed picture in the Kulkarni household. There was one before this, which Vaibhav had tucked safely under his handful of clothes, empty bags and academic files in the cupboard of his bedroom. That night, he pulled out that picture after years. It contained him in a silk kurta pyjama and a groom's veil made of flowers. Next to him was a woman in a bridal outfit with the traditional vermilion decorated on her forehead. No one other than Vaibhav had access to this picture. But if they did, they would be surprised at Vaibhav's ability to smile during better years. A large, thick crack ran diagonally across the frame of the picture. This had occurred when he had sub-consciously tried to damage the picture by sitting on it. On hearing the frame crack, he had felt a little guilty and had tried to convince himself he had sat on it by mistake. Then he had left the picture as it was, in the cupboard – some place where he would not have to look at it and yet would have easy access to when he wanted to. That night, years later, he still could not determine what he wanted to do with that wretched thing.

He took a quick look at it and muttered, 'I hope you are happy now.'

He was contemplating sitting on the picture once again when he heard a knock on his door. He quickly tucked the picture back under his files where it was meant to lie.

'Yes?' he responded.

Nisha opened the door and stood at the threshold in a night-suit she had quite grown out of. He observed that her pyjamas now only barely reached her ankles.

'We must buy you a few new pairs,' he noted, 'this Sunday.'

'Papa, there is something I want to tell you,' she said.

Vaibhav turned on the light in his room and tiredly sat on the edge of his cot. 'Of course. Go on.'

'I just wanted to tell you that I am not keen to celebrate my birthday at the farmhouse,' she said in a firm voice. 'In fact, I had no idea that Khurana Aunty would approach you with such a plan.'

'But it is absolutely alright even if you are keen,' he patted her. 'Why have you come here specifically to tell me this? In fact, you know what? The farmhouse plan is not that bad after all. We can think about it if you like.'

When he was her age, back in his town particularly, there were no birthday parties. The birthday boy or girl was given a new pair of clothes and was instructed to touch the feet of his elders to seek blessings. If the year had been fruitful enough, a bowl of rice pudding would be made after dinner. Boom. Celebrations done and dusted. But Vaibhav was not blinded to what a birthday celebration meant today. It was an event that was spoken about days before and after the party –

themes, budgets and caterers were discussed among parents. The children looked forward to an interesting surprise at every party – would it be a magician or a jester? Or a DJ for the slightly older children? He knew Nisha also went to such parties hosted by her friends. It was unlikely that a mind as impressionable as hers would not succumb to such fancies.

He pulled her closer and rested her face in his arms. 'Nisha, I know you want to have a memorable party. I want that too. I will talk to Khurana Aunty.'

She shook her head and looked downward. Twitching her lips, she replied, 'No Papa. I don't want Khurana Aunty to plan my party. I want you to plan it. I loved the party we had last year. Can we do something similar again this year?'

His throat grew a lump so large he feared she would see it. He hugged her hard until he was able to breathe normally. 'I love you,' is all he could utter.

'Good night, I love you too,' she said. He waited at the door until he saw her little silhouette walk back into her room. He then switched off his light and lay down on bed. Here was someone who could read right into his soul, and then there were some who never even considered his presence. A lava of overwhelming love, a little bit of hate, and the consistency of his frustration raged within him for a while. And then he sobbed himself to sleep.

A verse is all I have,
to take your heart away

A plate comes hurtling towards him like a flying saucer. He shields his face with his trembling hands. The plate goes crashing to the floor. The sound of porcelain cracking on cement tiles in the dead of the night is loud enough to awake the dead. He picks a piece of the broken crockery and studies the imprint on the rim: "Vaibhav weds Varsha."

'Congratulations, you have broken our first wedding gift,' he says dully.

'This wedding is broken, mister!' She screams. 'To hell with the plate. How dare you spy on me!'

Vaibhav laughs despite himself. He is not sure if he is losing his mind or if he has genuinely found her question utterly stupid.

'I am so sorry I managed to discover your true colours,' he says, and then adds. 'And don't you dare break one more piece of crockery in my kitchen.'

'Oh, get lost!' she yells at him and prepares to retreat into the bedroom.

'*Do not turn your back on me, Varsha,*' he yells back. '*You are answerable to me.*'

She turns around and comes charging towards him. His heart is in his mouth. She is in a fit of rage alright. He half-ducks to shield himself again.

'*BREAKING NEWS, Vaibhav! I am not answerable to you,*' she bellows. '*Do you want to know why? Because your own life is a bundle of unanswered questions. You are but a mediocre man who owns nothing but a piece of infertile land and a failed business. But listen now – you will not own me or my decisions, is that clear?*'

'*Very clear,*' he contains the large drops of tears forming in his eyes. His attention turns towards an infant's wail emanating from inside their room. He looks at his wife again. '*And what do you want to do about that, Varsha?*'

'*Your guess is as good as mine,*' she shrugs and begins to walk away again.

'*And that is all you have to say after three years?*' he asks after her.

'*This room is up in smoke!*'

'*I see. Wait...what?*'

'T his room is up in smoke, Papa!'

Nisha ran towards Vaibhav, who had just been caught lost in stupor. He had left the steam iron on her school uniform. He gasped and turned off the iron before examining the pinafore.

'Safe,' he grinned. 'And nicely ironed too. Here, take it and get ready.'

She took her uniform and scurried into her room. Two minutes later she emerged outside and went straight to the kitchen. Two slices of bread had been left warm on the pan. A fistful of grated cheese lay in a plate on the side. She layered her bread and ate in urgent gulps.

'Have you eaten?' she asked.

'I am all ready to go,' he replied.

She wiped her mouth and hurried to the main door. 'Let's go, then.'

'You are forgetting your tonic,' he pushed her back into the kitchen.

A piece of ginger in a cup of hot water was the said tonic. It worked wonders for the singing tonsils. And that evening was more crucial for him than it was for her. It was the evening of the Big Expectations From A Little Voice. She had won the inter-class singing competition the previous two years, and the stakes had only risen further. He shuddered to imagine how brittle a ten-year-old's dreams could be. Hence he had made her rehearse relentlessly through the nights leading up to the date of the contest until he was sure she was satisfied. He had asked Leena Madam to put in extra hours into her sessions. Leena Madam had gladly obliged. Everything seemed set.

'Are you confident?' he asked her for the zillionth time when they were en route to her school.

'Yes,' she replied, secretly wishing he would stop asking her that unnerving question so many times.

He gave her a good luck hug as he dropped her at the school gate, before riding on to work. Taneja had been duly informed by Vaibhav about his daughter's event in school and that he would like to leave early. Samar arrived at Vaibhav's desk and threw a fit about why *he* had not been kept in the loop about his leaving early that evening.

'I am leaving early this evening,' Vaibhav spoke in a flat tone without looking up from his screen.

'Well, thank you for letting me know after I have asked you,' Samar hissed. 'Come to the meeting room. I want to review the proposal.'

Vaibhav headed straight to Taneja's cabin instead of the said meeting room. Taneja raised a palm and asked Vaibhav to calm down.

'The Brazilian client is arriving today,' he said. 'We have just a few hours. Why don't you work this out peacefully with Samar and tolerate him for just half a day, huh?'

And hence it was decided. Vaibhav spent the next two hours in that meeting room tolerating Samar, imagining it to be some kind of gas chamber. Samar belted out one ridiculous phonetic correction after the other in the document, which he might have as well made on his own instead of dictating it. But wrapping up work in time for the day was higher priority than Vaibhav's ego that day. Hence he silently obliged. At the end of this scathing review, news came in that the Brazilian boss had mistakenly reached Chennai instead of Pune and would now grace the office with her presence only in the evening.

'I will not be able to stay back for this meeting, then,' Vaibhav reiterated his need to leave early.

'Taneja, isn't that anyway a limited audience meeting?' Samar asked, and then without waiting for an answer, turned to Vaibhav. 'You won't need to attend it. But please stay on call support in case we have technical questions to be answered.'

'I won't be taking calls either,' Vaibhav's tone rose in anger.

Taneja blinked his eyelids at Vaibhav in a plea to calm down. He then looked helplessly at Samar, who was now walking away gesturing to Vaibhav with his thumb and little finger over his ear.

'ON CALL SUPPORT,' he repeated mutedly as he disappeared out of sight.

Meanwhile, a strange phenomenon was unfolding at Goodwill International School. It all began when the Hindi teacher of the sixth grade presented her students with their marks of their internal exam. This being the last exam to have its marks declared, the results were totalled with great frenzy to reveal an astonishing result. Nisha had stood second in the class, lagging the top ranker by an appalling nine marks. The class teacher took her to a quiet corner after class to probe her for possible lapses. Nisha Kulkarni could not have stood second. This was not happening.

'I will do better next time, ma'am,' Nisha promised.

This was all forgotten soon, however, as the bell signalling the end of the last class went off. Students from various classes lined up to walk to the auditorium. The participants of the contest were ushered into the green room behind the stage. From a half-open door she saw the lights come on the stage. The orchestra had arrived and was setting up its instruments. The emcee, a teacher from the high school who was fairly popular among her students for the looker that she was, had just finished examining her make-up in her pocket mirror for the third time. Despite the loud chatter in the audience, Nisha could hear her heart throbbing wildly. She had been there before. She had won them before. But this was the first time she would be on stage before her father, and this changed the entire equation. His opinion mattered over that of the jury.

'I hope he likes it,' she whispered nervously to Bali.

'He will, provided he makes it in time,' Bali checked the time by his watch. 'Look, I am going to stand at the entrance of the auditorium so I can guide him in.'

'You are so sweet, Bali!' She pinched his cheek.

'Next time, please say that in front of your father,' he joked as he walked over to the entrance.

The competition took off shortly. Nisha was fifth in line. The first three singers had delivered stellar performances. The students at the rear of the auditorium were on their feet in applause. But her attention was still fixed at the entrance, which she could look at from the edge of the green room.

'Our next participant is Pratik Shah,' announced the emcee. Just then, an event volunteer from the high school section tapped Nisha's shoulder lazily. 'You are next.'

As Pratik Shah sang his last stanza, Vaibhav walked into the auditorium, escorted by Bali. He looked at the stage and whispered something to Bali. Nisha smiled in relief.

'No Uncle, she is next,' Bali whispered back.

The second and third rows of the hall were reserved for the parents. Bali had left his handkerchief on a middle seat of the third row to earmark it as "reserved". An uncooperative parent was now seated on his handkerchief, next to his uncooperative wife.

'Uncle, if you don't mind,' Bali leaned forward and whispered in the man's ear. 'This is the next participant's father. I had reserved this seat for him.'

The man pretended he had not heard, seen or sensed the presence of a boy breathing heavily into his ear. He continued looking in the direction of the stage. Nisha sensed the commotion and felt a tinge of discomfort on watching her father struggle to get a seat.

But Bali had not given up hope. 'Uncle, I had also left my handkerchief on the seat, no?'

The uncle's wife now glared hard at Bali. The uncle looked at Bali for the first time and exclaimed, 'Oh! Ok.' He lifted his bottom from the seat and pulled out a crumpled handkerchief like a magician pulling a rabbit out of a hat. 'You should take care of your belongings, son,' he said and then looked towards the stage again. Bali scanned both the reserved rows dejectedly. Everything was taken. His own parents were at the aisle of the second row. Students in the rows behind were tapping Vaibhav and Bali off their line of sight.

'It is alright, Bali, we can find another spot,' Vaibhav pulled the boy out of the row.

'Our next participant is Nisha Kulkarni from the sixth grade,' the emcee announced after Pratik Shah had walked off the stage.

The crowd erupted in deafening applause. Vaibhav first looked at Nisha as she made her way to the centre of the stage. Then he looked at the delirious audience in delight. 'GO FOR IT NISHA!' boomed a voice from some corner of the auditorium. Nisha looked at her father as the orchestra played a few random beats to mentally tune into the next song. Her eyes met her father's as he raised his thumb in a gesture of good luck. Bali pointed to some vacant steps next to one of the rows.

'Looks good, come on,' Vaibhav held his hand and both of them settled on the steps.

Nisha continued to look at Vaibhav even as the keyboardist behind her asked her if she was ready. *Why must you have to sit on the steps while the others get chairs*, she seemed to ask Vaibhav. *Don't worry about me, I have a wonderful view*, his eyes seemed to return a response.

'Nisha, are you ready?' the keyboardist prompted her once again.

Meanwhile, a security guard came running to Vaibhav and Bali. 'You cannot sit here.'

'Why not?' Vaibhav demanded.

'This is a fire exit row,' he explained. 'Please. You need to move.'

They were losing time. The orchestra had begun playing the music. Nisha searched her father's shadow as it slithered across the rows as instructed by the guard. They moved at least four rows further back and now squeezed themselves amid students who had occupied stairs in the central aisle. The orchestra had finished playing the prelude. She missed the note she was supposed to pick the vocals from. Frustrated, they played the entire prelude again. The audience looked at her in anticipation. She was still looking for her father, but he was out of sight now. She imagined him sitting in the sea of restless students who would be constantly jostling for space. They would elbow him, push him, ask him to duck. He must be uncomfortable, she thought. But she also thought he would be a lot more uncomfortable if she missed picking up the vocals for the second time. She had spent over forty seconds on the stage already. Another five seconds and she would be escorted off the stage.

The prelude ended. This time she picked the cue and sang *Shaayarana* from *Daawat-e*-Ishq. Miss Suzanne led the charge from the audience as she let go of staff appropriateness and let out a shrill whistle of appreciation. The students followed suit and erupted in loud cheer. As the orchestra would tell all participants later, 'It is a delight playing music for people who can do justice to our music!'

'ONCE MORE!' the crowd started chanting after she had finished. Vaibhav struggled to stand on his feet, around which young boys and girls were cuddled in clusters. 'Yes, once more!' He waved his hand frantically and caught Nisha's attention.

She waved back at him with a broad grin. 'I will see you in a while,' she gesticulated from the edge of the stage even as the next participant took the spotlight. Vaibhav tried striding forward towards her but his path was entirely blocked. He settled back on the staircase next to Bali until the results were announced.

'What do you think, Uncle?' Bali looked at him.

'I think she will win,' Vaibhav said, warming his palms to keep them from going cold and numb. 'What do you think?'

'I know she will,' Bali replied without looking at him.

Vaibhav glanced sideways at him and smiled. 'Good to hear that.'

She did win. As one of the judges said, 'No contest there for the first position – Nisha Kulkarni from the sixth grade.'

Vaibhav lunged forward. 'Sorry, sorry, sorry!' He alerted students who tried making way for him as he scampered down the stairway towards the stage. Nisha met him halfway up the stairs and got enveloped in his hug.

'There you are, the proud father!' Miss Suzanne joined them a few seconds later. 'I thought you had not turned up. You ought to be proud of this little girl.'

A few other teachers took turns to congratulate Vaibhav and to tell him how lucky he was to have a daughter as talented as Nisha. He beamed with pride until his attention turned once again to Miss Suzanne. He got reminded of what Nisha had told him the other evening at Pizza Hut.

'Thank you, Miss Suzanne,' he said. 'She has your guidance and encouragement to be backed by.'

'You are too modest, Mr. Kulkarni,' Miss Suzanne smiled graciously. 'But I will take that. Now I must ask you the question you have been evading for too long.'

'Dinner? Of course, Miss Suzanne,' Vaibhav nervously chewed on his parched lips. 'We do intend to come.'

'Let us put that down on our calendars,' she instructed him. He saw her pull out a diary to note a committed date. Miss Suzanne meant business.

'Er, Miss Suzanne, let us keep it after Nisha's final exams, you think?' He suggested.

She closed her diary with a sigh. 'This is the first dinner I am pencilling in three months in advance. Save the date, yes?'

Bali, who had been quietly watching the conversation with immense interest, commented. 'Ma'am, Vaibhav Uncle is a thorough gentleman. He will keep his word.'

Miss Suzanne studied Bali for a moment and then looked at Nisha for a confirmation. 'We promise, ma'am,' said Nisha.

'Alright then, I will meet you all again soon,' Miss Suzanne craned her neck in the direction of the other teachers. 'I have to attend a staff meeting before we call it a day. Please excuse me.'

'Of course. Bye.' Vaibhav said, almost relieved.

Outside the auditorium, they were met by Bali's parents. Ajit Khurana, just like his wife and son, was a man of fine taste in clothes and perfumes. He greeted Vaibhav warmly and congratulated him. 'We were rooting for Nisha all along!' he said, and then turned to Bali and told him it was high time he acquired reasonable talent in some extra-curricular activity other than Candy Crush. Bali sulked and tiptoed out of the circle of conversation before his laurels were discussed any further. Presently a bunch of students from their class came running from the other end of the corridor, screaming at the top of their lungs in congratulations. All of them collapsed in a heap upon his daughter even as Vaibhav looked at them frightfully.

'Are they your classmates?' he asked once the children had stood back up on their feet.

This was no less than the third time he was being introduced to them. But Vaibhav's ability to remember faces he was shown months ago was very limited. He usually compensated for this flaw by going out of the way to be friendly and courteous towards them.

'How are you, kids?' Mrs. Khurana asked before meticulously rattling off the names of all eight of them in quick succession.

'Ah, so nice to meet you kids,' Vaibhav said. 'I have been wanting to meet you so I can invite all of you to Nisha's birthday party at our apartment.'

A uniform look of disappointment showed collectively on the children's faces. They looked slantly at Bali's mother, who in turn looked at Vaibhav. Clearly the farmhouse idea was being floated for a long time already and a lot of hope had been built around it. But Vaibhav had the final word of approval from Nisha, who looked at him and nodded once again.

'Thank you for your offer,' he said to Mrs. Khurana. 'But I spoke to Nisha and she says it was a lot of fun at our place last year.'

Taken aback as she was, Mrs. Khurana nodded vehemently. 'Of course, of course. That was a mere suggestion. A home party is just as much fun, right kids?'

The kids were not amused. They looked at each other unhappily until they found Nisha giving them a tough glare.

'Nisha, do extend the invitation to all your other friends who aren't here,' Vaibhav told her. 'Tell them I have invited them.'

'Sure,' said Nisha.

'Uncle, it is a class of forty,' one of the students reminded him, just in case he realized his apartment was not large enough to host that number and then changed his mind in favour of the farmhouse.

'Do not worry about that,' he said. 'We will make arrangements. And don't worry about me spoiling your party either. It's just going to be you all and a lot of fun and food!'

He said goodbye to the children, shook hands with Ajit Khurana and grazed Mrs. Khurana's fingers once again.

'Papa, I will be with you in a minute,' Nisha whispered before joining her friends in a private conversation. Vaibhav walked up to the gate with Bali's parents as the children got into an important debate.

'I thought we had all decided on the farmhouse,' one of them complained.

'Nisha, try explaining to your father, no?' reasoned another. 'We were all so bored last year at your home party. There was so little room and so little to do.'

'It was not that bad,' Bali said, assessing Nisha's rising temper.

Nisha picked up her bag and prepared to walk. 'This is not fair, guys. It is my party and I don't like you telling me you were bored last year. This is how it will happen: the party is at my house. Those of you who would like to come are most welcome. Those who are not keen, feel free to exclude yourselves.'

She stormed out of the corridor, leaving her friends stunned and speechless.

I'm leaving on a jet plane

Two *boondi laddoos* were placed on Vaibhav's desk when he arrived to work one morning. They looked delicious and inviting. He proceeded to pop one into his mouth pronto. Then he realized it would be much politer if he first made enquiries about the giver of these delicacies and the occasion they were being distributed for. The employee in the adjacent working bay was polishing off one such laddoo himself. Vaibhav did not know his name; he only knew he was some kind of a maintenance tester.

'What is with these?' asked Vaibhav, picking the first laddoo and smelling it with much love.

Maintenance Tester smacked his lips in delight. 'Ah! You did not hear. Samar Yadav is the benefactor. He has apparently clinched a big deal in the Brazilian account. I heard the management sat him in its lap, patted him lovingly and requested him to lead a long-term assignment in Brazilian Exotica for his hard work on the proposal.'

Three. Two. One. The laddoo in Vaibhav's hand self-destructed into a sloppy mound of yellow. He spotted Samar's oblong head bouncing over some cubicles away as it nodded gleefully in acceptance of the incredible feat he had supposedly achieved singlehandedly. He considered his options: one laddoo still lay on his table. What were the odds he could take perfect aim at Samar's cranium from fifty feet afar? Would that amount to violation of corporate ethics? Would he care about the violation anyway?

Bhandari always had a ready solution to such dilemmas much like he did that day: QUIT. Throw your resignation in their filthy faces. You deserve better.

'That is a very crazy suggestion, thank you.' Vaibhav had taken to a corner of the pantry for an emergency telephonic chat with his trusted adviser. 'Unless, of course, you are willing to bear my home loan EMI till the time I get a new job.'

'I don't mean you QUIT, quit,' Bhandari corrected himself. 'I mean you metaphorically quit. Put in a word of resentment at least, man. Don't let them take you for granted – any more, that is.'

And so Vaibhav decided to quit metaphorically. He put in a word of resentment to Taneja wherein he stated that he was no longer happy being taken for granted. He also wrote that he would shortly put in his papers and his decision was nearly irreversible, because being jobless was better than not being given due credit for the work he was doing on his job. Thirty minutes later, just as Bhandari had prophesied, Taneja summoned him to his cabin.

'I have not received your resignation in my inbox yet,' Taneja spoke with a straight face. 'What is up?'

Vaibhav went pale, noting which Taneja broke into peals of laughter.

'No, I really did mean it,' Vaibhav rose to his own defence. 'I am very upset, if I can be honest.'

'Oh, come on, Vaibhav,' Taneja flapped a dismissive hand at him. 'Do you think a) I do not know quitting a job in one's mid-thirties is easier said than done, and b) I am some sort of stupid dodo who does not know what each of my subordinates is up to? The answer to both, by the way, is a big NO.'

'But…' Vaibhav began, but was cut in.

'Let me explain,' Taneja stretched as he got up from his chair, 'over a hot cup of coffee.'

He reluctantly followed Taneja to the Costa outlet right outside their office building. The café was well-occupied for its time, barely an hour before most employees went out to lunch. Frustrated and excited and conniving and naïve employees occupied various tables. From a distance they all looked the same, like cookies that had just popped out of a baking batch. But it was safe to assume they harboured various emotions right in the middle of another week (even the weeks over time looked like cookies from a batch). He stood next to Taneja in the queue at the counter, absently scanning the faces of every customer. He tried ignoring the happy faces and focused on the frustrated ones instead. They made him feel more at home.

'One toffee nut latte,' Taneja said once they were at the counter, and then looked at Vaibhav. 'And?'

'And,' Vaibhav replied without applying much thought, 'another toffee nut latte.' He held out his credit card which Taneja examined admiringly before pushing it away.

'Nice card, Vaibhav. Use it some other time.'

Vaibhav was too tired to protest. They stood quietly at the other end of the counter for their coffees to arrive. They held their respective mugs and took a table at the centre of the café.

'I love that card,' was Taneja's first remark. 'So how many free flights have you enjoyed already?'

'Free flights?'

'Did they not tell you?' Taneja flashed his own, almost identically abled card so he could explain. 'You score purchase points and redeem them against practically anything – including flight tickets. I redeem them mostly against my wife's monthly investment in overpriced shoes.'

'Ah!' Vaibhav pored over how many big ticket purchases he would have to make before he could book himself a flight ticket that he would anyway never use. Where would he take a flight to anyway? The only place other than Pune he had ever been to was Akola. And no plane had ever flown to Akola. He also wondered what Lady Taneja did with so much footwear. What did her footwear look like? He remembered Varsha had three pairs, more than most women in their neighbourhood: one dusty brown pair of sandals she wore with her sari, one pair of pink chappals with rose petal designs that she wore on her daily walk to the market, and a third pair of tennis shoes she had bought because she had complained her soles ached from all that walking to the market. She had been a beautiful woman. Slender in structure, ivory skin, and round hazelnut eyes that she had passed on to Nisha. Men admired her, women envied her. He remembered telling her once that she was so gorgeous she did not need branded embellishments to dilute her beauty. She had not believed him one bit. The same week some stranger on the road had told her she was so gorgeous she just had to try her luck in the film and fashion industries. She had believed that stranger instantly.

'Just make sure you minimize your cash spends hereon,' Taneja snapped him out of his unpleasant trip down memory lane. 'Use your card where you can. Make points. You won't believe what those points can get you, my good man.'

Vaibhav scooped the foam of his toffee nut latte with a spoon and gulped it disinterestedly. He then looked up at Taneja for a second before tilting his gaze beyond his shoulder.

'Ok, let it all out.' Taneja prodded him. 'Tell me the problem statement – Samar Yadav? Or lack of motivation?'

'Lack of recognition.'

'Lack of recognition, right,' Taneja pondered. 'I am going to change that right away. Take a look.'

He fetched a rolled up set of printouts from his pocket and flicked it across the table. Vaibhav took a glance.

"BRAZIL WORK VISA (TEMPORARY V) APPLICATION FORM"

He looked up, bewildered. 'You are welcome,' quipped Taneja with a wink. 'Now listen. This is what happened. We won a large engagement with the client, who was very impressed with Samar's pitch. We had to give Samar a large chunk. But we also managed to win a parallel data security contract with them, which I choose to nominate you for.' He paused, and then added compassionately. 'Kulkarni, you are a hard worker. You deserve this chance. The management was not convinced, given your role as a systems admin. I convinced them you are meant for progression. If you are proactive enough to extend a hand beyond your designation, it is only fair we give you this project.'

He caught Vaibhav lost in suspended gaze. 'Now don't tell me you are not interested. Dollars, Vaibhav, make life so much better. Think about it.'

Vaibhav recovered from his thoughts. 'Ah, no, thank you so much. I was just taken by surprise. Here I was wondering why my work on the proposal was not acknowledged. But you were two steps ahead of me already.'

'You don't *look* as happy as you sound,' Taneja considered him doubtfully.

'I am delighted,' clarified Vaibhav. 'But I am also a little jittery. It just means I will need to recalibrate a lot of things at home.'

Taneja slammed his coffee mug on the table and wiped his foamed moustache. 'Oh my God! Wait.' He pulled out a pen and wrote the word on a tissue: RECALIBRATE. 'That is a new one. Must use in the next meeting. Thanks.'

They both laughed, and just for a minute Vaibhav felt it was possible after all to take life easy and wait for the happy chapters to come by. But soon enough, he began worrying again. He was told the assignment would last six months with a fifty per cent chance of some extension.

'What will I do with Nisha?' he wondered aloud. 'She cannot possibly go on indefinite vacation with me.'

'She is a big girl, why does she need to go along with you,' Taneja began and then stopped short. 'But I will leave you for now with your personal matters and other required recalibrations. Tell me when you have made up your mind.'

They finished their lattes with more urgency now so they could get back to work. 'Can you give me until tomorrow morning?'

'Take until tomorrow evening if you must,' Taneja said as they walked out the door. 'As long as you answer in the positive. Keep the dollars in mind.'

It was an honest and wise suggestion. The dollars were to play a crucial role in his decision. But there were also some other important factors he needed to pay heed to. He paid a quick visit to *Goodwill International School* while Nisha was still in class. He waited an hour outside the principal's office before she allowed him a meeting. Introductions were polite but quick. Luckily for him, there was no shaking of hands involved. He was offered a seat and a glass of chilled water. The principal was in her mid-fifties. She wore a crisp cotton sari of a colour that suited her age. She had a pleasant face, but no smile. She also seemed the kind of person who liked coming to the point quickly. It turned out she knew Nisha but did not remember having met Vaibhav before. He did not bother explaining he had been present at all PTA meetings that far. Instead, he came straight to the point, explaining his dilemma and seeking her advice.

'We don't usually encourage unplanned long leaves for children,' she clarified at the outset. 'But I know Nisha has an impeccable track record and we can make an exception for her.'

'Will she be able to skip a term and progress to the next grade once she is back?' he asked her.

'Yes, but I am not sure that is all that must matter to you,' she took off her glasses and rubbed her tired eyes with the corner of her thumbs. Then she put them back on. 'Skipping a term is not the issue at hand. What will matter is the impact it can have on your daughter's confidence.'

He gulped and looked on at the principal, seeking elaboration. She sighed. 'Our curriculum, Mr. Kulkarni, look.' She lay out an array of colourful brochures like a deck of playing cards on the table. 'Six months down, the other students in her class would have acquired so much more knowledge than your child. Yes, she will progress to the next grade. But will she be the same student gushing with confidence, on top of her subjects? I wouldn't vouch for that. Unless, of course, you manage to find her a school in the new country that will be kind enough to admit her for a mere six months.'

He looked at her and smiled forcibly, acknowledging the impossibility of such a scenario. And then he silently mocked himself for the charade he was trying to put up before himself of offering his daughter a youth of prime education, limitless creativity and a sense of fierce independence. An independent child did not need to sacrifice her study term to accompany her father on *his* assignment.

As though reading his mind, the principal probed him. 'Have you considered the possibility of letting Nisha be? From what I have understood of her, she can make just as well of those six months all by herself – even if you travel. And then she has all of us at school to look after her if needed.'

Vaibhav looked at the watch by the table. He had exceeded the duration of his allowed appointment already. 'You are right, madam. She can look after herself alright. I was just not so sure I could say that about myself though.'

They both laughed and shook hands (which means, Vaibhav grazed her fingers with his) and then parted. He was promised Nisha would never find about this meeting and the purpose thereof. The siren of the electric bell was heard as he took the flight of stairs down towards the assembly hall, which indicated a class had just ended. Groups of students streamed out of the classrooms on the playground and on the see-saws and around the kind avuncular samosa-seller at the main gate, who sometimes offered a courteous child a free snack or two.

'Short recess?' Vaibhav stroked the hair of a boy, years younger than Nisha, who seemed to be looking for his friends at the bottom of a staircase.

'Yes,' the boy said, holding up a snack box as proof.

It smells of thalipith, Vaibhav noted, and continued in the direction of the gate. Closer to the bicycle stand, he noticed his daughter standing with her friends, their heads together in a discussion of utmost importance and excitement. He noticed the birthday invitation cards in some of their hands. He had sat with her late into the previous night at her study table. Braving fatigue and an army of moths attracted by the tube light, they had prepared these invitation cards using fancy chart paper and fragrant sketch pens. She was still the little girl he had seen a decade ago. But she was older than that boy he met at the staircase, older than many other students of the school.

Old enough to look after herself for six months, that was right. But the correct parental thing to do would be to let go of his short term gains and be by her side to ensure she maintained her focus ahead of her final exams. But the Brazilian project was not about his personal gains. It was about earning a good deal of money that would come in handy for her future. It was also about him earning a sense of self-worth he could write home about, which again was less about the self-worth and more about her being able to enunciate her father's achievements before her more illustrious friends. So what if that meant he would pull her off her schedule and her friends and her singing for six months or more? She would see a new country and come back smarter. But then she would grapple with the knowledge gap the principal rightly spoke about.

He carried this swarm of contradictory thoughts back to work. He reached his cubicle and looked at the visa application form lying on his desk. 'For the larger good,' he said to himself as he filled out the form, his fingers trembling with excitement.

Somewhere I belong

The maid came in an hour earlier as instructed on the morning of Nisha's eleventh birthday. The dining table had been relocated from the centre of the living room (there was no separate dining room) to the tiny passage between the living room and the kitchen. The rickety couch in the living room was moved inside Vaibhav's bedroom. One stubborn leg of the couch had come undone in the process. He left the limp couch and its abandoned leg in a corner of his room and made a note to fix the poor thing later that night.

'Use phenyl properly,' he reminded the maid frequently as she squatted on the floor and swept it in petite but expert movements.

She emptied half a bottle of phenyl into her bucket of water. Turning to Vaibhav, she asked hopefully. 'Baby's birthday, sir?'

'Yes, baby's birthday,' he replied. 'How did you know?'

She cocked her brows in the direction of an unopened packet of balloons lying on a chair. Vaibhav forked out a hundred-rupee note and offered it to the maid. 'For baby's birthday.'

'There she is!' she flashed a happy smile as Nisha emerged from her room, dressed in a floral printed dress.

'Happy birthday Nisha!' Vaibhav knelt before her and planted a kiss on her cheek.

'Thank you Papa!' she hugged him back, and then promptly looked over the shoulder. 'Is that a packet of balloons I see on the chair?'

'Twelve,' he confirmed. 'Enough?'

She suppressed a smile. The maid wished her 'Happy Birthday' which she replied to before returning to the discussion of the balloons.

'They are very nice,' she held the packet softly, 'but can we let them be today? We can use them later on some other occasion, you think?'

'No balloons at your birthday party?' he asked. 'Why wouldn't you have balloons?'

She held his arm and leaned on his side. 'Because, Papa, we had balloons last year and…and it was a little odd. Grown-ups don't have balloons.'

Vaibhav let out a throaty chuckle. 'Ah, did your friends give you a hard time for it?'

'Kind of.'

He laughed again. A car horn sounded below the building. 'That must be Bhandari Uncle. I will be back soon. Be ready, we will leave for school in a bit. And, alright. No balloons.'

He ran down three flights of stairs and greeted Bhandari, who was standing patiently outside his Hyundai Verna, dressed formally.

'In the car boot,' Bhandari stuck his thumb towards the rear of the car. Vaibhav opened it to find a set of Bose Speakers waiting for him. A compact music player on its side.

'You want me to walk them up with you?' Bhandari offered lazily.

Vaibhav balanced them all on his cradled arms. 'Nah, I should be…'

'Oho, easy, Hercules, take the bag,' Bhandari warned him. 'In the boot too.'

Vaibhav saw a neatly folded bag at the deep end of the boot. He carefully placed the speakers and the music player in the bag and beamed at his friend. 'You are always so thoughtful!'

Bhandari responded with a deadpan expression. 'I almost cried there. I don't want a speech. I want to have "the holy drink" with you. When can that happen?'

'Shh, quiet!' Vaibhav placed a finger on his lips and gestured towards his window on the third floor. 'Nisha must not hear of your habits.'

'My habit, and your occasional indulgence, right?' Bhandari bowed before him. 'So will His Highness oblige?'

'She has a party with friends at home this evening,' said Vaibhav. 'The house will be off limits for adults. Let us take to my terrace? Bring Old Monk. I have only Pepsi at home.'

'Pepsi is fine,' Bhandari winked. 'I will get the Old Monk hidden under my shirt. If Nisha sees it, I will drop it in your lap.'

Vaibhav pseudo-kicked Bhandari before carrying the bag back up home. The maid had sparkled the floor nice and squeaky clean. She had also cooked breakfast proactively for which Vaibhav reluctantly parted with another fifty rupees as Everyone Is Happy It Is Baby's Birthday bonus.

'Sir, you made these noodles?' She opened a bowl and displayed its contents.

'Pasta, not noodles,' Vaibhav took the bowl from her and placed a lid on it tightly. 'Nisha, it is for your party. This was all I could learn to cook. But I know you like pasta. Everything else has been ordered from outside – samosas, cake, chips, pizza, chowmein. If you can think of something else, give me a call from your smartphone and I will order.'

Nisha giggled. 'Papa, just call it a phone. And I can't believe you made the pasta all by yourself.'

'She helped me.' He held out a Tarla Dalal cookbook lying on the kitchen shelf.

They ate hurriedly and were on their way out soon. The maid would stay back and spread out the rented mattresses Vaibhav had rolled up and stacked against the wall. *Enough to accommodate three classrooms*, he told Nisha when she asked him if they would suffice. Fresh music CDs comprising Rihanna's latest albums and Rihanna's free pin-up poster along with one of them were placed by the side of the borrowed Bose speakers.

'Has Rihanna wished you?' he joked as they drove to her school.

'Yes, she wrote on my Facebook wall,' she joked right back.

He dropped her off at school, rode to office and worked like an efficient machine. Taneja had been waiting for his affirmative response on the Brazil project. But Vaibhav ducked the discussion – he would talk to Bhandari over Old Monk and arrive at a reasonable decision. For now, he laboured over a set of system reports as part of his obligatory weekly analysis to ensure that Synergy Software's infrastructure did not crash and that the company did not go kaput and that he would not be forced to try and set up that lousy garment business of his again. The caterers he had ordered food from had informed him that the desired quantities of every item had been duly delivered to the maid. He had chosen the caterers upon ensuring that each of them accepted credit cards for payment.

Later in the day, he called Rachna from the bank to enquire if he had collected enough points for any new freebies.

'Sir congratulations, you can avail of a new mixer,' she confirmed after tapping a few keys on her system.

His hopeful voice sank. 'Just a mixer? I have been using this card everywhere I can – except maybe at the tea stall outside my office.'

'Sir, you are funny!' She laughed. 'But keep using it, sir. Spend more, earn more freebies. Do you have the brochure I had given you? It has all details on redemption of points, for your reference.'

'I have the brochure,' he replied sadly. 'I just thought it will be quicker to check with you on the phone.'

'Any time, sir,' she assured him.

'By the way,' he spoke on a beat. 'Just out of curiosity – how many points do I need to make in order to get a free flight?'

'It depends on what sector you are looking at,' she tapped some more keys on the system. 'But in the range of twelve to eighteen thousand points for a domestic flight. And in the range of thirty to sixty thousand on an international sector.'

'Domestic is fine,' he said almost to himself, and then thanked her before hanging up.

He had all of eight thousand points after all those monthly spends he had made: the servicing of his motorcycle, the dine-outs, the occasional film with Nisha. And all he was being offered in return was a mixer. He grudgingly finished the rest of his work. At four-thirty, Nisha called to tell him she was on her way home with her battalion of friends.

'How are you all going?' he asked. 'Did you get enough cars?'

'Eight of them,' she said. 'When are you coming home?'

He factored in a long pending visit to The Royal Pune Club. 'I will be there in an hour. Don't wait for me. The food should be all set up on the table. The music player has come too. Put on some good music and get started.'

'Ok, come soon,' she said and hung up.

He digressed towards The Royal Pune Club on his way home. The same security guard was manning the gate again. They waved and smiled at each other as Vaibhav rode straight into the parking lot. With renewed courage, he strode up to the reception desk. Hair Gel was on duty and he looked as grumpy as he had the other day.

'Yes?' came the abrupt, direct question when Vaibhav walked up to him. No greetings were considered necessary.

'Ah, I wanted details of the membership here,' Vaibhav began uncertainly.

'Membership? Of this club?' Hair Gel's eyebrows converged like those of a werewolf. He turned on the Membership Eligibility Scanner installed in his head and considered Vaibhav from top to bottom. At the end of the exercise, he let out a short grunt and held out a semi-torn piece of paper. 'Here you go.'

Vaibhav saw a table filled with six-and-seven-digit numbers for half-yearly, annual and lifetime membership. He choked.

'Seen? What would you like?' Hair Gel prodded him with a know-it-all look. *You would like everything, but you ain't gettin' nothin'. I see your dilemma like I see the hole in your shirt, would you like to consider your finances first?*

Vaibhav cleared his throat. 'Actually, I don't intend to use all facilities of the club. I was only looking at using your pool.'

'Only the pool?'

'Only the pool,' Vaibhav nodded eagerly. 'And to begin with, only for a month. You see, I might be travelling abroad next month for a while, so I'd like to take it slow.'

'Ah, globetrotter,' Hair Gel noted disinterestedly. 'No sir, you are getting it all wrong. This is a very elite club. Very exclusive. And we don't negotiate on these rates. I can recommend a club in Pimpri, if you'd like to take a look. Much smaller, but I think they can help you with a customized swimming membership.'

'It will take me forever to travel to Pimpri everyday,' Vaibhav noted thoughtfully.

'That is too bad.'

'Can we strike a deal?' Vaibhav mustered whatever courage was left in him. 'I am very keen…' he noted Hair Gel's nameplate pinned to his chest: *Hasmukh* – he who is always jovial. Irony died a gruesome death that very moment. 'I am very keen, Hasmukh. I have been a swimming champion in school, hence the desire.'

Hasmukh smirked in a non-Hasmukh way. 'I played a lot of Pac-Man in school, sir. Do you see me designing games at Microsoft? No, I am a receptionist. I have even forgotten how to play Pac-Man now. I wouldn't recommend anyone to hold on to one's unfulfilled dreams. Real life is a lot different. Sit.'

He offered Vaibhav a glass of water, like he was about to relay a very devastating piece of news. 'A half-yearly package for a lakh. That is the best the club will offer you.' He found him looking dejectedly into nothingness, and added: 'I can understand what you are thinking about. I think about it myself all the time. *If only I could too*. We are the If Only I Could Too class, sir.'

What was this man's problem, seriously? Going on an overkill of unsolicited counselling with such power-packed emotions. Vaibhav needed to use the pool. He did not need counselling. Counselling was a farce. It never helped. It never filled the lacuna in anyone's life. He thanked Hasmukh for the water in the glass. Then he looked at the water in the pool and allowed yet another dream in his heart to implode. And then he was on his way home, convincing himself that this meeting never happened.

'If only I could have had a say in this entire episode,' she mutters. 'We both could have been spared this trauma.'

She lugs out her suitcases into the living room and catches her breath. 'I am leaving. Now is as good a time as any other.'

'Wonderful,' he replies. Having run out of energy to quarrel any more, he has settled on a chair. 'Let me know when your film releases. I might watch it.'

Varsha snarls. 'Just because you have achieved nothing, you don't need to be sarcastic about my ambitions. Wait and watch. I might just surprise you.'

'I will be waiting,' he replies mechanically. 'Please leave. I have nothing to say to a woman who can defy her husband after being lured in by some phony casting agent she has met on the road.'

'In case you are forgetting,' she gives him a stern gaze, 'I have won two beauty pageants before losing my way into your home.'

'Miss Kolhapur, I know,' he says. 'I saw the news tickers on BBC. I think they had flashed your photograph too.'

She thumps her feet angrily and drags her luggage out towards the foyer. A moment of realization dawns upon him. This could be it. His family is disintegrating. His daughter needs her mother. This cannot be happening. He runs after her; stops her at the door.

'Don't do this, Varsha,' he points in the direction of the sound of the wailing baby. 'Don't do this to our daughter. We can make things work.'

'I don't belong here, Vaibhav,' she lets go of his grasp with a jerk. Tears are streaming down both their faces. 'I had placed my faith in you. First the land, then your business. What is next? I see only imminent disaster. I need to find my calling.'

'Why would you give birth to a child only to abandon her like this?'

'Like I said,' she looked at him with teary eyes, 'I wish I could have had my say somewhere.'

'You will have to come back here, Varsha,' he cries out after her. He sees her slip out into the streets until he is blinded by the darkness of the night. Then he runs back inside to attend to his daughter.

Let 'em know
we are still rock n' roll

'This pasta tastes horrible!' exclaimed Sunaina of the Chanel nail-paint fame.

Nisha smiled. She owed one to Rihanna once again. *Hate That I Love You* played in the background, and Bhandari Uncle's Bose speakers were effective enough to drown out Sunaina's voiced opinion of what was indeed a very badly made pasta. 'Have more, na,' Nisha held the bowl towards Sunaina, who cringed and moved out of the way, back towards the rest of the gang. It was only when Nisha filled her own plate with the pasta that she realized it bordered on inedible.

'Nice pasta,' remarked Bali as he went for a refill of his Pepsi. 'Let Uncle know.'

'Shut up!' Nisha yelled into his ear, even as she couldn't help but be amused by the remark.

'The good news is that most of them haven't tasted it yet,' he said. 'You might want to take it off the table. We can handle it between ourselves.'

'You don't have to eat it if you didn't like it,' she said. 'There is pizza.'

Bali took the pasta off the table and faced the kitchen sink. 'It is not that bad after all. Yes, it is bland. The sauce is floating all over the bowl but has not stuck to the spaghetti. And Uncle has totally forgotten about the seasoning. But hey, there is ketchup.'

He squirted a litre or two of ketchup on the pasta, mixed it and held the plate up in the air. 'For friendship!' he raised a toast to her.

She followed suit and scooped a spoonful into her mouth. 'For Papa!'

'Mean.'

'That is how I roll.'

'Let us rock and roll,' he said, and moonwalked over to the other students sprawled on the mattresses.

Vaibhav arrived shortly. He was startled by the loud music, but he blended in when the kids came up to him in ones and twos and groups to greet him.

'Hope everyone is having fun,' he hollered. No one was able to hear him.

He stepped into the kitchen to monitor the consumption of the pasta. Nisha had placed the bowl in his view.

'Half empty already!' he peeped into it joyfully. 'Not bad, eh?'

'Not bad at all,' she said. 'Very nice, actually.' He had not observed, of course, that only two of forty plates had pasta in them.

'Give me your Just A Phone,' he demanded. 'And go sit with your friends. I will take some pictures.'

She did as instructed. Vaibhav positioned himself at various corners of the room and clicked a series of pictures. The students, oblivious to his exercise, continued chatting and shouting and singing. He gestured to Nisha that he would be upstairs on the terrace.

'With Bhandari Uncle!' he shouted when he saw a question in her eyes.

Bhandari reported on time with the said bottle of the holy drink. Vaibhav had spread out two folding chairs, sourced from the repository of chairs for the society's use – purchased by forking out Entertainment Accessories Surcharge from the owners. The sun was beginning to set. Tired housewives were seen pulling off dried garments from their clotheslines. There was a consistent flow of the evening traffic on the road below. Lemonade and juice hawkers were stepping up their sales pitches in anticipation of tired office workers stopping by to replenish themselves.

'The city has smelt and looked exactly the same every evening,' Vaibhav said, scanning his surroundings. 'Every single evening for the last four years.'

'Not sure cities are supposed to change,' Bhandari said. Two glasses were filled out, mixed with Pepsi and the drink that would not be named aloud. 'They are always the same. What do evenings in Brazil look like?'

'I do not know.'

'The internet tells me they look splendid,' Bhandari responded to his own question. 'Beach shacks, loud music, parties, pretty women. I have read Brazil knows how to have fun.'

'Good for Brazil,' Vaibhav quietly took a sip and looked out at the horizon.

'What have you thought about the offer?' asked Bhandari.

'I am going to decline it,' said Vaibhav, and then in the same breath added, 'and before you give me stick for it, let me tell you that it has been one of the most difficult decisions of my career.'

'Ok.' Bhandari joined Vaibhav in looking at the setting sun. He took tiny sips of his drink so he could linger on to its taste longer. He knew Vaibhav was not likely to go for a refill with his daughter in the vicinity.

'Ok what?' Vaibhav turned to him.

'Ok that I don't like interfering in your matters,' Bhandari explained. 'But if I were you, I would take Taneja up on that offer.'

'Ok.'

'Ok what?' asked Bhandari.

'Ok that I value your opinion,' Vaibhav replied. 'But it just did not feel right to uproot Nisha from her schedule. She stood second in her class in the term exams this time. Do you know that? For the first time in four years she slipped from the first rank to the second.'

'Peanuts?' Bhandari ripped open a packet and offered it to Vaibhav, who obliged with a fistful. 'How many students are there in your daughter's class? Fifty?' he continued.

'Forty.'

'Which means there are thirty-nine students in every term exam who don't get the first rank. That is an incredible statistic. You know what, Vaibhav? I am sure those thirty-nine students are turning out just right. Why are you being so hard on your own daughter?'

'I am not hard on her. I might be paranoid, yes,' he admitted. 'But it has been a long journey for me to bring her up to be this happy, intelligent, well-rounded child. I have slogged to make her study. I have put in all my might to enable her to pursue her singing classes.'

'You are a rockstar father, I know,' Bhandari leaned back in his chair. 'I know it takes a lot to rear a child. Maybe that is why my wife and I have delayed the decision of starting a family for this long. We are not even sure we want to go ahead with the decision at all. But you, my friend, are a rockstar.'

They poured themselves one more refill. Vaibhav went for three-quarters Pepsi in his glass.

'How does it matter? I still worry,' he said. 'I worry about her future. I worry about how she would feel if she were deprived of her ambitions or if she were denied entry to a premium club by some Hasmukh. I fear for her safety - and you know there is enough reason to be concerned.'

'But what about your career?' Bhandari spoke when he got a chance. 'This international assignment could change the game for you. Does that not matter?'

'It does to the point of being able to feed two mouths and to save for her higher education,' he said. 'I will pull that off somehow with what I am doing right now. Anything more than that will only mean I am trying to hold on to frills I don't really need. They are only desirable, at the most.'

'Desires are very desirable.'

'I don't know,' Vaibhav shrugged. 'My biggest desire as of today is to see a success story in her.'

'How would you measure that success?' Bhandari challenged him. 'Success is endless.'

'If she is self-sufficient and happy, she is successful,' he replied matter-of-factly. 'I don't want anyone to go to her and tell her she is a failure. Someone said that to me once. I know how it feels.'

'Don't mention your wife now,' Bhandari complained jokingly. 'It nauseates me.'

Vaibhav looked up from his glass and stared sternly at his friend. The mention of Varsha nauseated him just as much. But only *he* had the permission to say it aloud.

'Oh my God, sorry,' Bhandari stuck out his tongue. 'Touchy topic.'

'Forgiven,' Vaibhav winked. 'For the sheer fact that we stayed in touch even after you left Akola years ago. Had I not had you in Pune, I would be drinking Pepsi on this terrace alone tonight.'

They laughed. Then they talked some more until the sun disappeared behind the horizon and a starlit sky took over. Vaibhav got up only when he heard some car horns blaring near the gate of the building.

'I think the kids are about to leave,' he said, leaning over the parapet. 'I can see two drivers with their cars.'

'How do we destroy this evidence?' Bhandari held up the nearly empty bottle of Old Monk.

A little weighed in by the alcohol he was just not used to, Vaibhav's speech dulled a bit. 'Don't destroy it. Take it back with you exactly the way you had sneaked it in.'

He pulled up his shirt a little in demonstration. Presently footsteps were heard on the staircase leading up to the terrace. A rattling of the bolt and a creaking of the door.

'Now!' Vaibhav hissed.

Bhandari stashed the Old Monk under his t-shirt just in time before Nisha walked in through the door.

'Aye, is the party over?' Vaibhav stretched his arms to give his daughter a hug.

Nisha went into the warmth of his fold. 'Almost. Bali and a few others are still there. They will leave in a bit.'

'I made them pasta!' Vaibhav proudly informed Bhandari, who smacked his lips in delight. 'Is there any left?'

'Er, no,' Nisha replied, and then swiftly changed the topic. 'Can I use your computer?'

'Why?'

'I want to transfer the pictures from the party,' she said.

'Upload them directly on Facebook no?' Vaibhav asked, and then took her phone in his hand. 'Did you show Bhandari Uncle your Just A Phone?'

Nisha passed on the phone to Bhandari Uncle, who examined it with crinkled eyes. 'Ah. Nice phone. But the battery life is not that great.'

Vaibhav snatched it back from Bhandari's hand and gave it back to Nisha. 'Pessimist. It is a smartphone.'

'I want to transfer them to a computer,' she said. 'I want to share them on Picassa and it will be much faster to do it on your computer.'

'Ok, but don't touch any of my work folders,' he said. 'I am just having a short chat with Uncle. I will come home in a while. See your friends off till then.'

'Alright, good night Uncle!' She shook Bhandari's outstretched hand.

'Many happy returns of the day once again, princess!' he smiled at her.

'Thank you! Can I get you some cake?'

'No, thanks,' he patted his taut but slightly inflated stomach. 'Watching it these days.'

Vaibhav cleared his throat. 'I see.' He waited until Nisha had disappeared out of sight. 'Quit all this *daaru* and a piece of cake instead won't hurt.'

They bantered for a while longer until Bhandari feared his wife would blow her lid for his little bachelor-ish outing. Vaibhav walked him to his car, where they bantered some more before calling it a night. When Vaibhav returned home, the living room was all quiet. The used paper plates had been stacked neatly near the dustbin. The mattresses were folded and pushed back against the wall as they had been that morning.

'Everyone left?' he shouted out. No response.

He opened the refrigerator and saw she had kept two large pieces of cake for him in a tray. There were samosas and a lone slice of pizza too. But the liquor floating in his system forbade him from further indulgence. He picked one piece of cake and ate it while clearing out empty cardboard boxes and a few stray tissues with his free hand.

'Nisha?' No response.

He went into his room. She had turned off the computer after using it, but the transfer cable of her phone was hanging by the USB slot. He changed into his pyjamas and plucked out the transfer cable. The door to her bedroom was shut. He knocked on it lightly. 'Nisha!'

No response. 'Are you in the bathroom?' No response.

He drank some water and watched some television and ironed their clothes for the next morning before knocking on her door again. This time with some more fervency. 'Nisha. Open the door. Are you in the bathroom?'

Ok, thirty minutes. She was not likely to have been in the bathroom all that while. He felt a little uneasy. 'Where are your birthday gifts? I am waiting so we can open them together, beta.'

No response. No, wait. He heard something. He did not like the sound. It felt like a suppressed howl or a sniffle or maybe even a random burp. Like it had been stifled by allowing it to melt into the softness of her pillow. He rapped on the door harder. 'Alright now, open up. What is going on? You know the rules of the house. We don't lock doors.'

The sound grew heavier. Deep, muffled breathing interspersed with proper, disturbing whimpers. With that, the creaking of her bed. She was in bed already. Without having wished him good night. Without waiting for him to open her gifts. A ritual was being broken. The happy pattern of their household was beginning to rupture. He felt his head spin. He held on to the handle of the door and now started begging of her to respond.

'Are you crying? What's the matter with you? Come on, we can talk.'

Whatever it was, it had happened in a matter of under an hour. She seemed absolutely alright when he had seen her on the terrace.

'Open the door,' he spoke successively in tones of an order, a threat, and then a plea. She did not respond.

He was now sweating under his collar. Nervous, he looked around for help, almost forgetting he had no one to ask for help from. The knocking persisted until the crying inside stopped. A loud creak of her bed.

'I am tired, Papa,' she spoke finally. 'I want to sleep.'

'This is not the way you go to sleep,' he chided her. 'You haven't even wished me good night. Does it hurt to open the door and speak to me once? Now open up or else I will keep knocking.'

He heard the creak of the bed again. She was in bed again. She did not intend to open the door.

'This is unacceptable, Nisha,' he shouted. 'Just because I spoil you silly, you cannot take me for granted. Behave yourself and open the door. We don't lock doors. We don't sleep without wishing each other good night.'

She took a few seconds to gather a firm voice. 'Good night, Papa.'

He retreated as he spoke angrily. 'I see you have grown up. Is this about wanting your own space or something those other kids in your class talk about all the time? I will just have you know this will not work with me. We will talk about this tomorrow.'

He retired to his room and lay in bed for hours. He could not bat an eyelid. The sound of her suppressed cries haunted him. In the middle of the night he tiptoed to her door again. On hearing her light snores, he felt half a degree relieved. At least she was asleep. He lay back in his bed and took a couple more hours to bat his eyelids. It was undoubtedly the toughest night of his life. That far.

Cuts like a knife

The next morning he found her missing. Her birthday gifts from the previous night were stacked unopened on the floor. He could hear from the bathroom the patter of water drops fall on a half-filled bucket. A wet towel was thrown on the edge of her bed. Frantic, he ran to his room to try calling her when he saw she had texted him:

Needed to reach school early today. Did not want to wake you up. I took an auto.

He was tempted to give her a piece of his mind. But then he feared she would be thrown off focus during school hours, and hence decided against it. In the evening when he arrived at her school gate to pick her up as usual, he saw another message from her that read:

Going home by auto. Don't come to pick me up. Come straight home.

Alright, this was it. She needed a piece of his mind. When he got home he found her making herself a glass of lemonade in the kitchen. He had decided on his way he would be debuting as The Angry Parent that evening. But on seeing her innocuously going about her business like the little child that she was, he went back to starring as Daddy Be Mild.

'Is it my motorcycle?' he asked her gently. 'You don't like it anymore?'

There was no defiance on her face. But there was no intent to respond either. She hung her head low and walked out of the kitchen and into her room.

'Do you know there is a word in the dictionary one can use when one has done something wrong?' he followed her towards her room.

'Sorry,' she replied without looking at him, and was about to close the door when he held it mid-way.

'Come out,' he ordered with a flick of his finger. 'I want to talk to you. There is no need to run inside your room for nothing.'

She complied and followed him to the living room. He examined her vacant gaze. 'What is the matter? You look a little off since last night.'

'There is no problem, Papa.'

'Are you sure? You don't look like there is no problem.'

'No, no problem.'

He sighed tiredly. There was no point goading her continuously. 'Alright, bring your gifts. Let's see what your friends got you.'

She obeyed him. But he saw no excitement or resentment or any other emotion in her as they opened more than thirty gifts over half an hour. Finally, as the ritual went, he handed her the gift he had bought her – a set of twin Parker Beta fountain pens.

'Thank you, Papa,' she planted a kiss on his cheek. Finding him in search of approval, she scribbled her name on her palm and added. 'It is beautiful. Very light to hold, too.'

'Good,' he said, and later went on to instruct her. 'Nisha, don't do that again. Don't leave home without informing me. I always drop you to school. If you need to leave early, let me know. I can always wake up earlier. Ok?'

The next morning he felt happy to see she had stuck one of those pens against the pocket of her pinafore. All the other gifts, however, stayed untouched in her cupboard. Even the gift wrappers lay mangled among them in untidily shaped balls, away from his sight.

For the next two weeks, she went along with him on the motorcycle as they usually did. She spoke a lot lesser and her replies were sometimes curt too. But he had the consolation he was at least by her side. He dismissed her behaviour as an expected anomaly of a child who had just moved a year closer to adolescence. Of the few conversations they had over those days, he sensed withdrawal in her tone and her body language, like she was trying hard not to be, well, withdrawn.

'When do your term exams start, you said?' he asked her one Sunday morning while flipping through the papers.

'This Wednesday,' she replied without looking up from her book.

'Are you well prepared?' he asked her.

'Yes. But I need some revision.'

He observed her for the next thirty minutes. Not one page of that book had turned for all the concentration she seemed to be studying with. 'Take a break if you don't feel like studying. You have been on that page for long.'

She smiled sheepishly when he caught her bluff. 'Ok. Can I take a nap?'

He studied his watch. Eleven in the morning. 'This is a strange time for a nap. Anyway, keep it short. Lunch will be ready in some time.'

When he went to her room to wake her up for lunch, he found her lying on her side, open-eyed. 'You were napping while trying to study. You are awake when you were supposed to be napping. Are you sure nothing is bothering you?'

She sprang out of bed exaggeratedly, as though to demonstrate nothing was bothering her. 'No. Let us eat.'

The term exams went by in a flash. She summarized every exam with a vague, 'It was good'.

But in a matter of weeks, skeletons had started tumbling out of the cupboard. For starters, Leena Madam called Vaibhav one morning and made enquiries about Nisha. 'Where has she disappeared to?'

Vaibhav was alarmed. 'I don't understand. Has she not been attending your classes every Tuesday and Thursday?'

'Not for the last three weeks,' came the response.

'But I have been picking her up from outside your building!' he exclaimed.

'Unless these old eyes have started failing me,' Leena Madam reiterated, 'I haven't seen much of your girl recently.'

'I will talk to her about it,' he promised her.

Before he could talk tough to Nisha about bunking music lessons, a larger catastrophe had already befallen her in school.

'You all need to shape up,' declared Mrs. Das, their science teacher who always told her students there was scope for improvement – but not in the most motivating ways. She had a bundle of answer papers under her arm as she walked into class.

Excited whispers escaped the class. 'Papers, papers! Ma'am are you telling us our marks?'

'Yes. What are you so happy about?' she snubbed them. 'You children have shaken my belief in science. The highest score is forty-two on fifty. Shameful.'

Everyone instinctively turned towards Nisha. 'Must be you only!' some of them said.

She chewed on her nails nervously without responding. Mrs. Das began declaring the marks by roll number with short, irritated grunts – like she was being force-fed Benadryl with every answer paper she was thumping in the children's hands.

'Twenty-one on fifty…thirty-six on fifty…thirty-three… nineteen…why did you even write this exam…'

The student who had scored forty-two went forward with a jaunty walk to collect his paper. 'No need to smile,' she snapped at him. 'Feel ashamed of yourself. You have lost eight marks for nothing.'

Some more sermon was doled out before she shouted. 'Roll number twenty-three?'

Nisha stood up and strode forward to collect her paper. Mrs. Das looked on, baffled. 'You are roll number twenty-three?'

Nisha stopped in the aisle. 'Yes, ma'am.'

'Are you sure?'

The class looked on in surprise. 'Yes, ma'am,' she confirmed.

'Eleven…' Mrs. Das mumbled, and then said. 'Wait. Take your seat. Let me check.'

She took another look at the answer paper while Nisha stood near her desk anxiously.

Mrs. Das looked up again, this time even more shocked. 'Eleven. Eleven on fifty. Nisha? What is this?'

She held up Nisha's answer paper in horror as a series of loud, horrified gasps were heard in the room. 'Shit…Nisha? It cannot be…eleven? Haw…oh, no…'

Nisha looked embarrassed and frightened, but not entirely surprised. She quietly took her paper from Mrs. Das and returned to her seat, digging her face under her desk.

'There is no point of crying,' Mrs. Das grumbled.

Nisha looked up with a straight face. 'I am not crying.'

'That is very worrying, then,' the teacher contradicted her own advice without realizing it. 'I would be crying if I were you.'

She waited till all the students had a good sympathetic look at Nisha. 'Do you know your score is the lowest in the class?' she mocked her. 'Even Mihir Modi has scored more than you. I can't believe my eyes.'

With one clean slingshot, Mrs. Das had insulted a certain, unsuspecting Mihir Modi too. The boy had the undisputed distinction of being the lowest grader in the class, year on year. 'Eighteen, right? Mihir Modi?'

Mihir Modi nodded sadly. Mrs. Das turned to Nisha again. 'Be careful. You have been a class topper. Now you are being the next Mihir Modi. This is not nice.'

The class laughed – barring Nisha and Mihir Modi, of course. Their otherwise harmless laughter felt like an array of swords scathing her insides. She hid away her answer paper in her bag and somehow held her own until the class ended. There were two more classes after Mrs. Das', but she could not wait longer.

'Papa, I have gotten free already,' she called her father and waited for him outside the gate.

He picked her up and drove her home in silence, gearing up to have a long discussion about her mysterious absence from her music classes. She threw him off-balance before he could start speaking, when she handed him her answer paper at home.

He had changed into his pyjamas and was crouched at a corner of his couch, crestfallen. 'Eleven on fifty?'

She held her head low. She had nothing to say. Yes. There was a big "11" written on the right top corner of the paper. There was no contesting that truth.

'Why, Nisha?' he made her sit next to him, trying to be that gentle parent who would get to the bottom of this by way of kind motivation. Inwardly, he was gutted. 'What happened here? Were you not prepared for this exam?'

'I made some silly mistakes in the paper,' she replied weakly. 'It won't happen again.'

'You cannot lose thirty-nine marks because of silly mistakes,' he said. 'You did not study well. Were you overconfident?'

'No, Papa.'

He shook his head disappointedly. 'Nothing else explains this. A class topper has just failed a term test.'

'It won't happen again,' she repeated. 'I am sorry.'

'Nisha, this is not the only thing I am unhappy about,' he added. 'I want to know if you have been hiding something from me.'

'No, Papa!' she shook her head firmly.

'How are Leena Madam's classes coming along?' he asked.

'They are good,' she fiddled nervously with the end of her pinafore. 'We…are learning *Raga Bhairavi*.'

'I spoke to Leena Madam this morning,' he cut her off. Every word of her lie cut like a knife. 'She said you haven't been going. I pick you up from outside her building twice a week. Where do you go during the class if you are not at her place?'

Nisha bit her lips nervously. Her eyes welled up with tears.

'I won't be angry, I promise you,' he comforted her. 'Just tell me the truth.'

'Nowhere,' she said.

'Nowhere? You stand outside her building and go nowhere?' he asked suspiciously.

'I sit in the garden across the lane,' she stammered.

He felt his tone rise. He made a mental note to keep it in check. 'Do you go to the garden alone?'

'Yes.'

'Why?'

She took a minute to muster the courage to respond. 'I don't like going to the music class.'

Her answer left him reeling. He struggled to react to that shocker. 'You…you don't want to learn music anymore?'

'No, Papa.'

'Do you know what that means?' he asked her angrily. 'It means you don't have it in you to be another Rihanna.'

'I know,' she said, this time a little defiantly, as though she couldn't care less.

He got up quietly and walked towards his room. She could see the dejection on his face and in his movement.

'Papa? I am sorry,' she called after him.

He responded without facing her. 'I have nothing to say to you.'

She felt the loud slam of his door slap her senses. An hour later, he found a piece of paper saying "SORRY" slipped in through his door. He picked it up and went out to her room. She lay vacantly in her bed. On seeing him next to her, she sat up straight.

'Why do you think you failed your science test?' he asked her again.

'I will score well in the finals,' she said meekly.

'That is not the point,' he said. 'I need to get to the bottom of what is happening. Your aloofness, this sad face, skipping music lessons, and now this science test – I can see a disturbing pattern. I want to understand the pattern. I don't care about this test, for now at least.'

She did not reply. He sighed. 'Alright, I won't talk about it. I can see you don't want to. But if we are not going to talk, it is going to get very difficult for both of us. Think about it.'

'Papa, please don't worry,' she attempted to pacify him.

'I will stop worrying the day you start smiling again,' he said. 'Meanwhile, remember one thing: you are not skipping your music lessons again. That is non-negotiable. Am I clear?'

'Yes, Papa.'

'Good. Now help me lay dinner.'

Questions of science, science and progress

'Hey, Nisha!' a voice was heard in the hallway outside the classroom.

Nisha turned around. Rupali, a keen competitor whose favourite pastime was comparing her exam results with Nisha's, was approaching her with an army of her trusted friends.

'Hi, Rupali.' Nisha knew Rupali nurtured a special kind of hatred for her. She did not hate Rupali back. But she did not care much about her either.

'I heard you scored an eleven in the science test,' she said. 'Sorry to hear that.'

If she was fed up of discussing her science test results, Nisha did not let it show. It had been a week since Mrs. Das had rechristened her Mihir Modi The Second. But girls like Rupali could not get enough of the joke.

'I heard so too,' Nisha replied placidly. 'But you don't need to be sorry about it. Wasn't your fault.'

'We were just curious, though,' Rupali said, and her friends giggled as if on cue. 'Where did you score those eleven?'

Bali came sprinting from across the gallery in his friend's defence. 'Look who is talking! Rupali, here's a reminder – you are not exactly Isaac Newton yourself. You scored only thirty. No great shakes, ok?'

Rupali smirked. 'You didn't need to run that fast just to tell me that, Bali. Be careful. You might lose some weight.'

'Chuck it, Bali,' Nisha said, pulling him away. 'Let's go to class.'

'Go. Take your bodyguard along,' said one of the girls from the group, to which they all laughed again.

'Ignore them,' Nisha whispered to him.

'I don't care about them,' he said. 'But what is wrong with you? Why have you been so grumpy of late?'

'I am talking to you, right?' she turned her head towards him. 'That should be enough.'

'Don't give me attitude,' he snapped. 'Your father also called me to check on you. He asked me if you have been acting randomly these days. I said yes.'

'Are you mad?' she retorted. 'Who asked you to say yes? I am totally fine.'

'Which totally fine student scores an eleven in science, man?' he asked. 'You also bunked three science classes this week. Mrs. Das was livid. She found out you were present in school and had attended all other classes. Do you know she has reported this to the principal?'

Nisha went white. 'Who told you that?'

'She herself did,' he replied. 'She told everyone in class yesterday, like it was the new budget announcement or something. She asked us to let you know.'

He saw her worried face, and said. 'Now get inside class. Mrs. Das has the morning session with us. Just try and be attentive today. She might forget about the complaint.'

Students streamed into the classroom at the sound of the morning bell. Mrs. Das followed soon after. For a moment Nisha thought the teacher had aged significantly since she had last seen her in class. The classroom looked like an estranged friend too. She once sat in the front row in the teachers' line of sight, the apple of their eyes. She had now failed one science test and had just about scraped through in the remaining exams. She had stood twenty-eighth in a class of forty. Not all the teachers had come to hate her because of it. But she had lost the privileged position of being the apple of their eyes. For Mrs. Das in particular, she had become more of an eyesore.

'You were the subject of discussion in yesterday's staff meeting,' Miss Suzanne had informed her late the previous evening, summoning her to the staff room. 'Darling can I do something to help? If you have difficulty understanding some lessons, our teachers can put in extra hours for you.'

Nisha had declined the offer and had assured a concerned Miss Suzanne it was a passing phase. But as she sat now in the science class after a sabbatical of three bunked lectures, she could feel it in her bones she was headed for more trouble. No sooner had she finished contemplating her situation than the irritable Mrs. Das caught her staring out of the window at a peepal tree.

'Nisha!' she heard a voice boom across the room.

She snapped out of her thoughts and turned towards the teacher who was waving her hand to grab her attention.

'Nisha will explain osmosis to all of us,' Mrs. Das declared. Nisha had no idea where that had come from. The only reference was that of a large flower drawn on the blackboard – complete with its symmetric petals and perfectly shaped leaves. And a stem that ran along the vertical axis of the board.

Nisha knew she had been cornered. It was too late to stage a headache or to pretend to squint with concentration at the blackboard or to plead guilty of napping. She went for the best possible option. 'I don't know, ma'am.'

Those now familiar whispers of "Oh, no" resonated across the room.

The teacher glared at her sharply. 'Where are our manners, Nisha? Need some fresh induction, do we?'

Nisha realized she had sinned. She had responded to a teacher without having gotten up from her seat. She made amends and stood up. 'Sorry, ma'am.'

'Now, the answer, please,' the teacher repeated. 'Explain osmosis.'

What part of *I don't know* had she not understood, Nisha wondered. She spoke again. 'I don't know, ma'am.'

She felt a sea of heads turn in her direction again. She heard the collective sound of students shifting uneasily in their seats. Restless whispers in the class from eager beavers who knew the answer and wanted to score with the teacher. Desperate class participation, FOR THE WIN!

The teacher turned red in the face until she resembled a neon bulb. 'Why don't you know? Are you a DUFFER?'

Some students laughed. Hearing someone being called a duffer is understandably funny – as long as you are not that someone, of course.

'Shut up!' Mrs. Das shouted at them. 'Did I ask you to laugh?'

The students quietened, waiting eagerly for the teacher to wave the Please Laugh flag.

She drilled her spectacled eyes into Nisha's again. 'How will you know anything? You have become so smart now you think you can bunk my classes and get away with it. And now I find you staring out the window. What was the subject of your interest outside the window, if I may ask?'

So now, looking out of the window was a constitutional crime. 'I was staring at this real plant outside the window, ma'am, not your phony drawing on the board. It was helping me understand osmosis better,' was what she could have considered saying. 'Nothing, ma'am. I am sorry,' is what she actually said.

'Sorry is not good enough,' the teacher grumbled. 'I know you have been bunking a lot of classes these days. I saw you in the play area yesterday, when you should have been in my class. What were you doing sitting under that tree? Were you waiting for an apple to fall on your head? Do you think you are Galileo Galilei?'

'Ma'am, Newton,' someone from the class spoke, and then the voice trailed off.

'Who said that?' Mrs. Das screamed.

A boy at the back stood up. Mrs. Das shifted focus on him. 'Do you want to leave the class with her? She is leaving anyway. Do you want to go too?'

'No, ma'am,' he said shamefacedly. 'I was just saying the apple had fallen on Newton's head, not on Galileo's.'

The class could no longer hold it. They burst into peals of laughter. Mrs. Das tore out her lungs once again.

'Nisha, enough,' she said. 'Tell me right now: what is osmosis? Otherwise leave the class.'

'I am sorry, ma'am,' she repeated. 'I don't know.'

'Does anyone else in the class find it difficult to explain osmosis?' Mrs. Das looked around. Half the class began belting out the answer in loud, insistent voices.

'Shh, quiet. Did I ask you for the answer?' the teacher shouted. 'What is this, some fish market?'

Nisha looked blankly at the teacher, shifting easily across her feet and also idly wondering if noisy fishes in the water were ever asked, 'What is this, a classroom?'

Mrs. Das turned sharply to Nisha again. 'Get out of my class. Right now. You anyway like it more outside.'

She slipped out of her desk nimbly and walked. On her way out, Mrs. Das realized she was not done venting out her anger just yet.

'And listen up,' she called out. 'If you think you are very intelligent, you will be in for a surprise in the final exams. You scored eleven in the terms, right? I dare you to pass in the finals. Just wait and watch.' Turning to the class, she announced. 'I will treat you all to a popsicle if she passes the Science finals.'

Nisha did not wait for the drama to end. She walked out of the classroom calmly, trying to ignore the hiss of "DUFFER!" that escaped Mrs. Das' mouth once again. She went to the merry-go-round behind the basketball court. Once she was certain she was alone, she broke into a helpless howl, wondering how to pick up the pieces of her scattered self-confidence. For now it looked like she was sliding down and there was no turning back up.

'What's the matter with you?' Bali came and sat next to her at the sound of the recess bell. 'Drink some water first. Then speak.'

She gladly gulped large sips of water. Taking a breath, she dabbed her face with her forearms. That left large brown marks of grime mixed with tears all along her face.

'Now speak,' Bali said.

'I don't know.'

'You said that twice in the science class today,' he said. 'You saw what happened because of that.'

She was about to start crying again when he held her hand gently. 'Listen yaar, I am really bored now. You haven't spoken properly to me in almost a month. I even need your help in completing my geography assignment. And here you are, moping day in and day out over God knows what.'

She forced a smile. 'I can help you with your geography assignment. Come.'

'Not like this,' he sprawled next to her. 'First tell me why you were crying. I want to help.'

'I will tell you someday,' she said.

'Oh, suspense! Ok,' he said. 'Have you had lunch?'

They heard the dribble of the basketball. The sounds of tiffin boxes opening in quick succession near the court. Students were pouring out of their classrooms for the lunch break.

'No. Shall we go?' she asked.

'Of course. Just. Do not. Cry. Ok?'

'Bali,' she said.

'Yes?'

Instinctively she wrapped her arms around him. 'Thanks for being my friend.' She leaned her head against his shoulder. It gave her comfort. A harmless gesture that should have stayed the way it was meant to be. Instead, they heard some whistles in the distance.

Bali retracted from her unforeseen hug and looked over her shoulder. 'Shit.'

A group of students from their class had witnessed the hug. There had been nothing dramatic about it. But imagination, just like innocence, courses generously in the veins of little children.

'Oye hoye, how sweet!' hollered one of the students, and the others laughed.

Bali turned angrily at Nisha and snarled. 'Are you mad? Look what you have done!'

Without waiting to gauge her reaction, he turned to his classmates. 'Aye, nothing like that, guys! Take it easy.'

'Ha ha, look at his cheeks,' they commented. 'He is blushing so much they are looking like Kashmiri apples!'

'Don't be shy, Bali!' screamed another. 'You two look great together!'

Nisha was in tears again. Bali, meanwhile, was busy salvaging lost pride. 'Wait, I will tell you how shy I am.'

He went running after them. Laughing and screaming, the students dispersed and scuttled out of his sight. He U-turned and came charging angrily towards Nisha.

'Congratulations,' he panted, resting his hands on his knees. 'Thanks to you, we both are going to be the subject of gossip all over school.'

Globules of tears as big as her swollen eyes ran down her cheeks. 'Bali, I…I didn't mean to…'

'What Bali, I…Bali, I?' he snapped. 'You don't have any common sense or what? We are friends, alright? You don't have to try and be my girlfriend. God, this is so embarrassing.'

She stood up in half a mind to land a slap on his fleshy face. 'Shut up, Bali! Don't you dare talk to me like that.' Her voice quivered like it was on the verge of dying.

'You shut up!' he growled. 'Now stop staring at me like that. Go and fix this misunderstanding before those useless fellows go running around school to tell everyone what they saw.'

She crossed her arms over her chest in defiance. 'I will not go anywhere.'

He placed his hands on his waist. 'Fantastic. I will have to clean up on behalf of you. Well played. Just remember we are not friends any more. You psycho!'

'Yes! A pyscho, and a duffer!' she trembled violently. 'GET LOST! I don't need a friend who can't be a friend when I am sad.'

'You and your sadness can go to hell!' he turned behind to yell at her one last time before walking away.

She tried to stand up. But she could not feel her feet. They had turned numb. She felt dizzy. Slowly, the blood moved upwards from her feet to her brain. *This is osmosis,* she said to herself. She bunked the Math class right after the recess.

'You need to take cognizance of this matter,' the Mathematics teacher secretly reported her absence to the principal.

'Maybe she is keeping unwell?' the principal hazarded a guess.

'I saw her loitering around the canteen five minutes before class,' said the teacher. 'She looked hale and hearty to me.'

'I will look into it,' said the principal worriedly.

During the short recess the next day, Nisha was making her way to the classroom when Rupali & Brigade intercepted her in the hallway again. This time, there was no Bali to help her either.

'Nisha, we hear you had a fun recess yesterday!' Rupali chuckled.

Nisha tried ignoring the comment and walking past the gallery. But Rupali was not one to be discouraged by the lack of attention. 'Was it just a hug? Asking because I wasn't there to watch.'

The other girls in the group giggled like magpies. The maturity quotient of Class 6 had just dipped to alarming levels.

'Can you leave me alone?' Nisha begged of her.

'Girls, can we leave her alone?' Rupali asked her friends, to which they all shouted, 'No!'

'Not until you give us some fun gossip,' Rupali goaded her. 'Tell us, na. Was it just a hug?'

'Yes,' Nisha replied quietly. 'It was just a hug.'

'Those guys told me she and Bali were whispering something to each other,' one of the girls reported to Rupali.

'How nice!' Rupali turned to Nisha again. 'Details, please?'

'Maybe Bali was telling her the definition of osmosis!' someone said, and they all burst into laughter.

'Is that right?' Rupali teased her.

Nisha turned to face Rupali. 'No, it was something else.'

'Tell us, tell us!' Rupali demanded excitedly.

'I can't tell everyone,' Nisha said. Her palms felt cold. She rubbed them lightly. 'Lean in. I will tell you in your ear.'

Rupali turned to her friends for approval, who encouraged her to go ahead. She leaned in a little. 'Ok, tell me.'

'With pleasure,' retorted Nisha, and with a balled fist she socked Rupali in her right eye.

The girls screamed in fright and scattered away.

Don't cry, child, you've got something I would die for

After a limited dose of appreciation for having worked on the Brazil proposal, Vaibhav was back to filing data archives on his desk.

'Well done,' someone from the senior management had patted him thrice on the back before handing him a Café Coffee Day Voucher For Two as a token of appreciation. He had carried that voucher to the closest outlet and had ordered two espresso shots for himself.

'That felt rich,' he had muttered to himself before returning to work.

He was glad Samar Yadav had disappeared to Brazil. He was upset that Samar Yadav still occasionally demanded his help with the odd assignment. But he had reconciled to the status quo.

He crossed paths with Taneja frequently on the office floor. All Taneja had ever communicated with him ever since his decline of the Brazil project was a cryptic, 'Hmm.'

'Good morning, Taneja.'

'Hmm.'

'How are you Taneja?'

'Hmm.'

'Taneja, there is an earthworm in your coffee.'

'Hmm.'

Well, almost. But the cold vibe was evident. Not like everyone at work otherwise greeted him with warm hugs and sloppy kisses. But he was beginning to get a feeling he had rubbed an otherwise kind-hearted boss the wrong way. This was only his secondary worry. His primary worry was his daughter. As though to accentuate the worry, he received a phone call as he was walking back to his office after consuming his espresso shots.

'Mr. Kulkarni, this is from the office of the principal of Goodwill International School,' said a voice.

Vaibhav's heart sank into the depths of his gut. 'Yes?'

'Putting you through,' the voice said and instantly the line was transferred to the principal. She began with a deep sigh. 'Mr. Kulkarni.'

'Yes, ma'am?'

'Please report to my office by three this afternoon,' she said. 'It is about your daughter. We need to talk.'

He tried containing the fear rising in his voice. 'Is everything alright?'

'Wouldn't be on the phone with you if everything were alright,' she replied tersely. 'Your daughter has been getting very aggressive recently, among other things I am unhappy about. Please make it here without fail, Mr. Kulkarni. The school would have initiated disciplinary action against her by now. But it is Nisha we are talking about, so we want to give her a fair chance.'

'But what has she done?' he asked.

'3.00 pm, Mr. Kulkarni, thank you,' she said and disconnected the call.

Vaibhav looked at his watch. Two hours to go. He spent them in his office, tottering around like a headless chicken. Then he rode to the school, his vision blurred by the tears stinging his eyes. When he arrived at the principal's office, he found Nisha sitting on a bench outside, expressionless. As though she was outside a movie hall, idly waiting for the show to begin.

He placed his hand on her head to comfort her, almost keen to place the other on his own head too. He could use some comfort too. 'Do you want to talk?'

She shrugged lightly. 'I think the principal is waiting.'

'Let's go.'

'I have been asked to wait outside,' she spoke as if to her toes.

Confused, he opened the door to find the principal seated in her swivel chair, her chin resting on her folded palms. She was listening with sympathy to a woman a few years younger, who was dressed in a short kurta (FabIndia, maybe), linen pants and a pair of nude pumps in her feet. A Louis Vuitton bag was slumped over her shoulder. A girl stood next to the woman, her hands politely crossed over her torso. Vaibhav had only a partial view of the girl's face.

The principal noticed him and nodded. 'Come in, please. Meet Rupali and her mother. Mrs. Verma, this is Nisha's father.'

'Look at this,' Mrs. Verma promptly held Rupali by the face and thrust it towards Vaibhav.

'Hi Rupali,' Vaibhav said nervously. He saw a purple patch around Rupali's right eye, like someone had splotched a ripe jamun on it. 'What happened to your eye?'

'Ask your darling daughter,' the mother suggested bitterly.

'Nisha punched Rupali earlier this week,' the principal said sombrely. 'This is not nice, Mr. Kulkarni.'

'Not nice at all,' agreed Vaibhav, who was visibly shocked. 'But she is a little girl. Rupali, are you sure Nisha gave you this colour?'

'What are we discussing here, a rangoli competition?' the mother demanded angrily. 'Look at the cut below her eye, mister. That maroon cut inside the purple colour, as you like to call it!'

'Yes, yes, terrible.' Vaibhav could not believe what he saw. 'Rupali, how did it all happen?' Turning to the principal, he added. 'I am sure you know Nisha won't do anything unprovoked.'

'We were just teasing her,' Rupali said softly.

'Why?' Vaibhav demanded suddenly. 'Why did you have to tease her?'

The mother threw her hands up in the air. 'Is that a justification for doing that to my child?'

'Mr. Kulkarni, please,' the principal intervened. 'No amount of teasing warrants such violence. Not in this school, no.'

She gave him a stern gaze. He pleaded, 'At least let her in and hear her out. I am sure there is more to it than meets the eye.' He suddenly looked at Rupali's swollen eye and noticed the rage on her mother's face. 'Sorry, didn't mean it that way.'

'I won't hear her out, Mr. Kulkarni,' the principal shook her head. 'You need to counsel her. That is all I can tell you. A drop in her grades, a drop in attentiveness, bunking of classes, and now *this*. Something is not going right, I can assure you.'

'I should have known better, actually,' Mrs. Verma commented suddenly.

Vaibhav looked around. 'I am sorry?'

'You should be,' she said, her eyes bloodshot. 'You should be sorry for not teaching your daughter enough manners.'

Vaibhav stood up from his seat, flying into a fit of fury. Mrs. Verma almost cowered with fright. 'How dare…,' and then realizing the inappropriateness, leaned back in his stance.

'No, Mr. Kulkarni, I know your kind very well,' Mrs. Verma said, struggling to recover from that brief scare. 'You only know how to show aggression. Like father, like daughter. Did you see that?' She looked at the principal.

'Why is she instigating me?' Vaibhav looked around helplessly. 'How dare she say that about my daughter? Listen, Mrs. Verma. I am proud of Nisha. I apologize for what happened to Rupali. But I am proud of my daughter. Do you hear that?'

'Please, adults,' the principal slapped her table in protest. 'Please. This is not a Newshour debate. Mrs. Verma, don't get personal. Mr. Kulkarni has apologized to you on behalf of Nisha. What more do you want? Medical compensation?'

Mrs. Verma smirked. 'Medical compensation? Really?' Glancing sideways at Vaibhav, she snorted again. 'I'd be damned if *I* were to ask *this man* for compensation. It will be an accomplishment for him if he can just teach himself and his brat of a daughter some class and culture. Or maybe even that's asking for too much.'

Vaibhav's fists balled with rage. He released them and clenched his armrest as he spoke to the principal. 'Madam, I am leaving. I did not know this was intended to be a fest to humiliate me and to show me my class.'

The principal raised a hand. 'Mrs. Verma, please take Rupali and leave. You have got what you needed. Please.'

He waited till the woman had walked out with her daughter. The clock had started ticking. There would be no more trickling of tears. An explosion, like the bursting of a dam, was in order. 'Can I leave too?' he asked.

'I am sorry about what she said,' the principal spoke softly. 'It was not in good taste. Thanks for bearing with that bit.'

Vaibhav stood up, ready to leave. 'It is easy to mistake one's helplessness for resilience, madam. If it weren't about my daughter's future, I had plenty to say to Mrs. Verma.'

He did not wait for a response. He walked out the door. Nisha had strolled towards the rosary outside the administrative building. When he went up to her, he saw she was in tears.

'I won't go to school from tomorrow,' she sobbed, burying her head in his chest.

'Let's go home and talk,' he held her by the hand and led her out.

Just short of their residence was a beautiful multi-purpose park ensconced in a quiet residential lane. Joggers took to its mud tracks. Parents, some of them in their official attire, brought their toddlers there to play on the slides. Aged men and women stretched on the park benches, examining everyone around them with due admiration or derision.

'Let's take a walk?' Vaibhav suggested.

Her silence meant compliance. He drove into the lane and led her inside the park. They walked two rounds of the track, allowing the gentle breeze and the chirping of birds to put their gloomy day behind them. He then bought her popcorn from the vendor near the gate. They took to a bench in the lawns and ate as they talked.

'So you don't want to go to school?' he began cautiously. 'Why?'

'You saw what happened there,' she cried. 'They are all mean people. They just declared I was wrong, without listening to me even once.'

'Yes, that was bad,' he conceded. 'But it was also bad that you hit that girl. That is most unlike you.'

'But Papa, she…'

He raised a hand. 'First admit you were wrong in hitting her. I will hear you out after that.'

She turned her head away in protest. He was sensing a rising simmer of defiance in her. 'Nisha, you are eleven years old. You are grown up enough to now understand that people will not always be the way you want them to be. Situations in life also are not always to your liking – be it your exam results, your being pulled up by your teachers, or your father being pulled up by your principal.'

'I am very sorry,' she spoke in a whimper. 'You had to get dragged into this because of me.'

'I am happy to pay a visit to your principal's office every day if that can make you a wiser person,' he held her hand in his. 'Nisha, receiving a complaint against you is the least upsetting thing that has happened in the last month.'

'I will not fail again, Papa,' she promised him. 'I am working harder on Science. I swear.'

'Failing the science test isn't the most upsetting thing either,' he said. 'Failure is a temporary setback and can be recovered from, sooner or later. I am concerned about your attitude of running away from difficult situations.'

'Papa, I feel very upset at school,' she complained. 'The teachers, Mrs. Das in particular, have started picking a bone with me over almost any and everything.'

'Don't they pick a bone with other students as well?'

'Not as much as they do with me,' she insisted. 'Every time I walk into class, I know someone is going to say something awful to me. It has become a daily affair.'

'Don't your friends stand by your side?' he asked.

She fell silent. Her expression said it all. He shook his head. 'And you were happy with this same school, this same class, when you had been topping every exam and were every teacher's favourite child? That is exactly what I mean when I say you are running away.'

'Please,' she was ready to cry again. 'Please don't make me go to school. I will study from home. Can you just request the principal for me to go on sick leave?'

'And what about Leena Madam's classes?' he changed the topic. 'What do you want me to request her for? Because I know you are still not attending her classes. I found out from her.'

'I am fed up of learning music,' she said in exasperation.

He shook his head, scanning the foggy air around him, wondering what to say next. 'You don't realize what you are saying. You might think now that you are fed up of the one thing you truly loved. Years later there is a good chance you will regret having got fed up of it. And by then you might lose the chance or even the intent to revive your interest in it.' Beat. He seemed lost in a time left far behind, and then added: 'Nisha, the failures in your life can never weigh heavier than the burden of your regrets. I have been there. I know what it feels like to have lost out on something you once thought you were born to do.'

'What did you lose out on?' she asked, staring at his pained face.

'I loved swimming once,' he confessed finally. 'I was a state champion during school. Did I never tell you?'

'No,' said she. 'Why did you leave it?'

'Why are you leaving music?' he countered. 'My reasons were not too different. But I can tell you there is nothing I regret more than giving up swimming. Do you want such a regret too?'

'No.'

'Then heed my advice. Get back to Leena Madam's classes, beta,' he persuaded her. 'You will realize its value much later. But you will know I was right.'

'I will, Papa,' she assured him. 'I will attend Leena Madam's classes regularly.'

'As well as your classes in school,' he added a sub-clause in the agreement, in response to which she instantly cringed. He continued: 'Time changes every point of view. If you trust me on what I said about regrets, trust me on this too. When you grow up and remember these days, you will know that this was a *great* school. Mrs. Das was not half bad a person. Failing a science test was not the end of the road. The students who teased you for failing will be standing on the same competitive pedestal as you once you are out of school.'

'Can I take a break, at least?' she pleaded. 'I can resume school after the exams.'

'No, you cannot,' he replied firmly. 'You will go to school from tomorrow. If you are scared of going alone, I will come with you till your classroom. In fact, you know what? I am going to wait outside your school gate all day. You just need to promise me one thing.'

'What is that?' she asked.

'Go to school with a positive mind tomorrow,' he said. 'If someone or something troubles you tomorrow, remember that I will be standing right outside the gate. You just need to walk out and you will find me. But just *try* and sail through the day. You might just discover it was not such a big deal. Can you do this much for me?'

She shrugged. 'I don't know.'

'I am standing behind you like a rock,' he cupped her head in his hands. 'There is no reason for you to fear. Just say yes. You will have a good day at school tomorrow. Say it.'

'I will have a good day at school tomorrow,' she repeated mechanically.

We don't need no education

'Did you see that?' Vaibhav squealed excitedly, pointing towards the television set perched on a wall of The Blue Nile.

He was lunching with Bhandari at their favourite haunt after ages. The ordered portions of food had substantially reduced since the last time. Vaibhav had lost his appetite and was mostly nibbling only on the cut tomatoes provided as a side, his chicken lying mostly untouched. Bhandari was still watching his paunch and so he had ordered only two naans with the chicken gravy, and had repeatedly requested for them to be ladled with less butter.

'Yes, I keep seeing that,' Bhandari craned his head to watch the news piece in question. 'Bipasha denies being romantically involved with anyone at the moment. She is in her happy space. That's nice.'

'Not that, boss,' Vaibhav clucked his tongue. 'Check out the ticker on top of the screen.'

Above Bipasha's happy face ran a news ticker. Bhandari read it out loud. 'Pop Sensation Rihanna To Tour Down Under. Hmm. And your point is what?'

Vaibhav did not respond. The news piece on Bipasha had just ended after the journalist was reasonably satisfied the actress was single. The next news clip was of Rihanna addressing a group of journalists outside Frankfurt international airport. Behind the barricades, an ocean of fans was waving at her frantically. He imagined Nisha standing behind those barricades. No. Knowing Nisha, she would have broken through the barricades and lunged at Rihanna like a fan-girl. What a moment that would have been.

'Nisha has always wanted to meet this woman in person,' Vaibhav spoke slowly.

Bhandari cleared his throat. 'I know. You have told me before. What do you have in mind?'

'I am wondering if I can take her to this concert,' Vaibhav replied instantly, almost without thinking.

'Down Under?' Bhandari asked, wide-eyed. 'That means Australia, mate.'

'Thanks for telling me,' replied Vaibhav. 'You look surprised.'

'No, no, I am just…ok, I am slightly surprised,' Bhandari confessed. 'Sorry I didn't mean to judge you. I just never thought of you as the guy prone to impulse purchases.'

'This is not an impulse purchase,' Vaibhav rued. 'I think Nisha needs a break. This could be the holiday she needs.'

'How is she doing now, by the way?'

'She is no better,' Vaibhav said. Bhandari was the only person he could confide in, and he had discussed Nisha's changing behaviour weeks ago. 'That sheen from earlier seems missing. She also looks low on confidence and morale. I think her teachers are giving her a hard time.'

'We don't need no education,' Bhandari sang.

Vaibhav returned a blank stare at him, and then added. 'She idolizes Rihanna. If she sees her role model in blood and flesh, in front of her, she could draw some fresh inspiration in life. And if nothing else, it will be a change in surroundings and all that.'

'There will be millions at that concert,' Bhandari said doubtfully. 'I am not sure how closely she will be able to take a look at Rihanna's flesh and blood.'

'What if I take her to meet Rihanna in person?' Vaibhav thought aloud.

Bhandari chuckled. 'Come on, man. I understand your feelings, but let's be a little realistic. That is not going to happen.'

Vaibhav frowned. 'I can read your real suspicion. You think I won't be able to afford that trip, don't you?'

He flushed a deep red. 'Who am I to decide that for you? Of course, if I were you, I would check the fares very carefully. Australia is an expensive trip any time of the year.'

Vaibhav stopped eating. Placing his head in his greasy hands, he broke down. 'What have I done wrong, Bhandari? I have worked hard all these years. I have worked honestly. But it never seems to be enough. Why do I have to think a hundred times before planning a trip for my child? This struggle never seems to end.'

'Ok, easy does it,' his counsellor offered him a tissue. But Vaibhav wasn't looking. His shoulders trembled violently as he sank his head into the table.

'Hey, I didn't mean to discourage you,' Bhandari patted him. 'Look, there will be a way out. We can work out this trip.'

Vaibhav broke down again, this time more inconsolably. When people around them turned to him curiously, he tried burying his face and his howls in his hands. And then his howl grew louder.

'Easy, man, easy,' Bhandari desperately tried quietening him down. 'I told you we will work something out.'

Vaibhav shook his head, writhing in pain. 'No! I think I had gravy stuck on my fingers and I now have chilly in my eyes! *I cannot see!*'

After enormous levels of ruckus had been created, he was taken to the wash basin and his eyes were cleaned up. He lay back on his chair with his eyes closed now, the tears mixing freely with the droplets of water that had settled on his face.

'Feeling better?' Bhandari asked a little later.

'The eyes have survived,' he said softly. 'Everything else is ruined.'

Bhandari slapped his forehead in frustration. Any more counselling would only make the man go more hysterical. 'Kulkarni, you don't have to worry about anything. I am there to help.'

The bill arrived. Vaibhav lunged at it and insisted on footing it. 'I have no doubt about your willingness to help. But if this trip has to happen, I have to make it happen all by myself.'

'You don't need to be so pig-headed about it,' Bhandari said.

'I am not being pig-headed,' he replied. 'I have always been an average person, Bhandari – unlike you. I was average when we were together in school. I am an average person now. I stayed average when you left Akola and pursued an MBA and God knows what else. This trip is the first opportunity I have got to do something special. I am thinking of taking my daughter to meet her role model. If I can pull this one off – all by myself – I will have at least one thing in my life to write home about.'

'Call me if you need any help,' Bhandari said. And on that agreeable note, they parted for the day.

It took Nisha a few days to be convinced about the arrangement proposed by her father.

'How can you wait outside the gate all day long?' she asked doubtfully.

'I don't mean I will stand,' he clarified. 'There is a café just across the road from your school, right? I will be very comfortable there. I'll pick up a book or a newspaper. Don't worry about me.'

She thought for a moment and then agreed. The last week they had spent at home together had made her at least moderately responsive to him. He had kept shorter hours in office that week, which had not gone unnoticed by Taneja. But it was at least getting him his daughter back. She still did not talk much. But she at least looked at him, watched *Indian Idol* with him, and forced a smile sometimes when he said something funny. His presence outside the gate seemed a reasonable assurance to her, and he was relieved to observe that.

The next day, he took no chances. He took the day off work and lingered around the school all day. At the end of every class, she strolled outside the gate to check if he was indeed around. Not once was she disappointed.

'Spying on me, huh!' Vaibhav joked when she stepped out after the third class that morning. 'I am right here. Is everything alright so far?'

'We had a surprise quiz on Oliver Twist in literature class today,' she said.

'And?'

'I scored eighteen on twenty,' she said, and smiled a little.

'Wonderful!' he offered a handshake, which she accepted. 'Was that the highest score?'

'No, someone got twenty,' she replied.

'That's ok,' he said. 'You can get twenty next time. What time is your recess?'

'After the next class,' she said. 'I got to go. The teacher must have entered class by now.'

'Run along,' he waved at her.

'I will join you for lunch during the recess,' she turned around to say.

'No way,' he said. 'You carry on with your classmates. I will have my lunch later.'

'I don't *want* to eat with my friends,' she said tiredly as though she had explained her stand on this matter a million times over already.

'Of course,' he relented, trying to conceal his worry.

He spent the hour leading up to the recess in the café. The news of Rihanna's upcoming concert in Australia gave him the tingles. He had looked up her itinerary on the internet: The Sydney Opera House, followed by the Rod Laver Arena in Melbourne, and then further down in Auckland. He had also clicked the *Ask Rihanna Your Questions* hyperlink in desperation and had asked her if she was planning a concert in India any time soon and that his daughter would be ecstatic if she could meet her once and that he could do absolutely anything to see his daughter ecstatic at that moment. He was not surprised he had not received Rihanna's response so far. But he now felt it was a good idea to take matters into his own hands.

He called Rachna and asked her how close he was to booking free round trip tickets for two between Mumbai and Sydney.

She spent some time on the call, examining airfares on her bank's website. She continued chatting with him as she went through options. 'I will suggest, sir, that you book your tickets via us instead of going through a travel agent. We will get you cheaper tickets and better redemption of points too.'

'So, did you find me any good news?' he asked hopefully.

He heard her breathing on the phone line, and then finally she spoke. 'I am very sorry, sir. You are falling short as of now.'

'How much?' he asked.

'You need another eleven thousand for a round trip for one passenger,' she said. 'For two, you need almost twenty thousand more.'

Vaibhav gulped an entire glass of water in one shot. 'And a one way trip?'

'Five thousand more,' she said.

No hope. Useless credit card. He wanted to get it out of his wallet and slam-dunk it into the trash bin near the café's billing counter. 'Ok, thanks. I will let you know once I have figured out something.'

The only big ticket purchase he could think of immediately was Nisha's school fees for the next year. And that payment was still three months away. He had lunch with Nisha an hour later, and then went to the administrative block to enquire if he could make an advance payment towards the next year's school fees.

'No one in the history of our school has come to us with a request of that kind,' said the officer sitting behind the desk. 'We will only be delighted.'

'And do you accept credit cards?' Vaibhav flashed his card before his eyes.

'Anything that gives us money,' the officer grinned and accepted the card to process the payment.

Vaibhav returned to the café with renewed vigour but then learnt those points take up to two days to reflect in one's account. He sat out the rest of the afternoon until the final bell of the school went off and he saw his daughter – calm and sadness-free – walk out of the academic building.

'Did all go well?' he asked her.

'Yes.' She mounted the pillion.

He followed the same schedule the next day. Only, he brought his official laptop along so he could get some work done alongside. Nisha still stepped out occasionally to check on him on the sly.

'Still here!' he would assure her each time.

But the frequency of her visits outside the gate reduced on the third day. That day onward, he lingered around the café until the morning assembly had ended and the children were marched off to their classes. Once he was certain she was inside her class, he would quickly steal a ride to work so he could show his face to Taneja – who was still giving him the Hmm Treatment. By lunch, he would unfailingly be back at the café, waiting for Nisha, leaving no traces for her to discover he had been sneaking out of his promised jurisdiction.

'Do you want to go out for dinner tonight?' he asked her about a week later. They had skipped tiffin that day and had bought sandwiches from the café – with the credit card, of course.

'I am not so sure,' she said. 'There is homework.'

'We will go after you are done with it,' he insisted.

She agreed but showed no excitement about it. At the end of the recess when he was walking her back to the gate, he saw Bali trying to sneak out of their sight hurriedly, back towards the academic building.

'Hello, Bali!' Vaibhav called out. He was pretty certain the boy had seen both him and Nisha and had chosen not to stop by.

Bali flicked a glance for just a brief second, then changed his mind and pretended he hadn't heard the callout in the recess' noise.

'What was that?' Vaibhav turned to Nisha, confused.

'He has gone deaf,' she replied in a flat tone and walked away without bothering to elaborate on that obvious cold vibe all three of them had just felt.

At dinner later that night, he was not any better equipped with a decision on the intended Australia holiday than he was a week earlier. But Nisha's continued silence had got the better of him.

'Do you know Rihanna is touring Australia in April?' he initiated the conversation. 'Melbourne and Sydney, I think. And then she goes to New Zealand.'

She had finished her dinner before he had even begun eating. 'I didn't know about it.'

There was silence in the still air. That halting moment before you utter something that you know will weigh very significantly on your life in good time. *Don't say it, don't say it.* He tried curbing that raging voice in his head. But it did not stop warning him.

'When do your final exams end?' he asked her after battling that inner voice for a minute.

'The last exam is on the second of April,' she said, and then looked up at him. 'Why?'

That same stillness in the air. The same halting moment. *Shh, quiet. Don't say it, don't say it*, said the inner voice once again. *There will be no turning back from here. It will be a promise you will not be able to break. Don't say it.*

'Because we are going to Australia after your exams,' he said.

Hit me, baby, one more time

'What did you say you want?' Taneja looked up from his laptop in a frown. 'Leave? Why are you asking for it now? You have been on leave all this while in any case, no?'

'I didn't get you,' said Vaibhav.

'No. *I* don't get *you*,' this was the angriest Taneja had ever been with Vaibhav. In his defence, he had some strong reasons to be so. 'You have been practically on leave the whole of last month. I hardly see you in office. When I do, you are barely around for a few hours. And now you are putting in a formal leave application?'

'I know you are upset with me because I could not accept that project,' Vaibhav said. 'But I had constraints.'

'Constraints are all you have had since the time I have known you!' snapped Taneja. 'But there is only so much that I can co-operate with you in understanding your personal constraints. This company does not function on the basis of your mood. I was in the line of fire for placing my trust in a man who ended up declining a project of that importance.'

'I apologize for that,' Vaibhav replied. 'There is nothing more I can do to make up for what happened.'

'How long do you need to go on leave?'

'Two weeks, in April,' said Vaibhav, and then added with flourish like he was being extremely thoughtful: 'That is why I have approached you well in advance.'

'Oh my God, thank you!' Taneja mocked. 'Two weeks? I don't know if you have bothered to consider who will backfill you while you are away for two weeks. Where are you off to, if I may ask?'

'I am taking my daughter to Australia,' he said. 'To…'

'To?'

'To meet Rihanna,' he completed sheepishly.

Taneja threw his hands up in the air. 'I can't believe I am having this conversation. Now what do you want from me?'

'If you could approve my leave request,' Vaibhav continued in the same tone, 'I would be much grateful.'

'So you are giving me a choice?' Taneja studied him. 'Well then. My answer is no. I can't approve your request. Much as I have valued your contribution to my team, I need to take a stand where I think you are pushing your luck too far.'

Vaibhav smiled. 'Pushing my luck? Ok.'

'You won't play victim with me right now, Kulkarni,' Taneja challenged him. 'Is there anything else you need from me?'

Vaibhav stood his ground defiantly. Taneja sighed. 'You are going on leave either way, aren't you? I see you have made your plans already.'

'Yes, I am sorry,' Vaibhav cocked his head to one side. 'I have made a promise to Nisha. This trip is important for her.'

'So you have just taken me for granted,' Taneja noted, clearly livid. 'Walked into my cabin simply assuming I would approve your request, no questions asked.' Beat. 'Fine. Go. What do I say? Just remember these leaves will stay unapproved. I am afraid these things can come in your way during your appraisal.'

'I have free time these days,' Vaibhav told him. 'I also wanted to check if you'd like to utilize me for any additional work you'd like to delegate to me. I would like to be productive at least while I am around.'

Taneja softened a little; breathed easy. 'Then you be this nice guy and force me not to be upset with you. Ok. There is a new deal we are working on. We need some animation done on a few slides. Can you help?'

'Of course,' Vaibhav replied eagerly. 'Just let me know what exactly you are looking for.'

'I have a call in five minutes,' Taneja examined his Guess watch. 'Can we sit around two-thirty?'

Vaibhav's jaw dropped. He shifted uneasily in his stance.

'You won't be around at two-thirty?' Taneja examined him with suspicion that was slowly giving way to a new bout of anger.

'I have a passport appointment scheduled for Nisha,' he said, but was quick to add: 'But I can come back later in the evening and work on your slides.'

Taneja slapped his forehead with one palm. With the other, he waved Vaibhav out. 'Forget about it.'

'I really can,' he insisted.

'Vaibhav, this call is important to me,' Taneja pointed at his watch. 'Just like that Australian holiday out of nowhere is important to you. Bye.'

At two-fifteen, Vaibhav stood outside Nisha's classroom, seeking the teacher's permission to whisk his daughter away. He saw her on the last bench in the row farthest from class. She was angled away from the teacher's line of sight, almost as though the teacher was perched on one of the branches of the tree outside the window. He noticed two other students in the class: Bali, who was seated at comfortable distance from Nisha and was still trying hard not to notice him. And there was Rupali, whose jamun-shaded eye had gotten a little better but still stood out in the class like bright coral.

The teacher looked at Vaibhav, then at her with disdain, as though she had been interrupted mid-speech at the Red Fort.

'I must have you know, sir,' she said, 'that we do not appreciate interruptions mid-class.'

There were hushed whispers in the class. All eyes were on the duo that had defaulted on discipline. Nisha stood up hesitantly; it took her nearly a minute to register her father's presence outside the classroom.

'I am sorry,' he apologized. 'She has a crucial appointment at the passport office. She must come along.'

The teacher turned her head in the other direction. 'Nisha, the last I remember, this classroom had not been acknowledged as a public park that one can walk into or out of at will.'

Giggles in the room. The ones that embarrass you, shame you, hurt you – although they are just giggles.

Nisha stared coldly at her teacher. That expression could have meant anything: *Hello Lady Blah-Blah. Meet me, my name is Miss Deadpan. You are such a square, by the way.* All she said was, 'I am sorry, ma'am. I forgot to tell you.'

'Leave. I am going to mark you absent in the roster,' declared the teacher victoriously. Nisha merely hung her head low in response and walked out, her bag strapped over her shoulders. *Congratulations. You have the last laugh. Another absentee marked is another feather in your flamboyant cap.*

'Ma'am, Bali wants to leave too!' shouted some hidden face from the class, and everyone except Bali and Nisha burst out laughing.

Bali stole another quick glance at Vaibhav and then dug his face under his desk with a major sulk.

Vaibhav pretended he had not seen the joke in that comment. 'Let me take that,' he took the bag off Nisha's shoulders as they walked down the stairway and out of the school premises. 'What class was it?'

'I don't…Geography,' she spoke as though she had to struggle to remember.

Nothing of what he saw of her in that classroom seemed right. She had forgotten to seek prior permission to leave school early. Bali was avoiding her – and him too, of course. And it was certainly not Geography she was studying, staring out of that window. There did seem some merit in the complaint teachers were beginning to have against her – except Miss Suzanne, of course, who had met him on his way up to the classroom and had assured him Nisha was no less of a darling just because she had given Rupali a large eye and had missed some classes.

They arrived at the passport centre before he could ask her any further questions. Two distinct queues were formed, snaking all the way out of the administrative building on to the barren compound. Office-goers, newly married couples, pesky children and harried parents had filled into the spaces provided by the serpentine steel barricades provided for the queue formations. Clouds of hot dust were being kicked up by bored children who had sneaked out of the barricades and had found purpose in flinging dirt at each other. Not surprisingly, there seemed no clarity which of the two rows they needed to get into in order to get the applicant's picture taken. Vaibhav stood holding Nisha's hand in the middle of the two rows, softly making enquiries about the row he needed to join.

'This one,' a lady shouted out. She had a son, maybe two or three years old, in her arms. And a disinterested man by her side who silently leaned against the steel bar as he watched Vaibhav and Nisha join them in the endless wait to get inside the building.

The lady took to Nisha instantly while her husband merely continued scanning Vaibhav with no evident purpose.

'Would you like some water?' she took out a bottle for her son from her bag and offered it to Nisha first.

'Thank you.' Nisha accepted it gratefully before extending it towards Vaibhav. 'Papa?'

Vaibhav shook his head and passed the bottle back to the lady. 'Thank you, ma'am.'

Fifteen silent minutes passed. Vaibhav was conscious he had stayed rather quiet in response to the lady's courteous gesture. What could he give her son in return? He had no bottle of water on him. *Sonny boy I have nothing to give you except these stress lines on my forehead. Or maybe a prayer that you be a happy person? Or wait. Take my id card. Take it. I don't want it. I demand you take it. Go, become the new systems administrator of Thankless Ltd.*

'Very crowded,' was all he could muster at the end of fifteen minutes.

'Very,' the lady nodded. Her husband had stayed quiet all this while. But his continuous gaze at Vaibhav was more unsettling than his silence. *Quick, involve the man in the conversation. He is feeling either left out or terribly insecure.*

'Hi,' Vaibhav said to him, in response to which he got a brief nod.

The line snaked forward a little and everyone breathed heavily in temporary relief. That took the responsibility of being social with his newfound friends off his shoulders for a while.

Ten minutes later, the lady smiled at Nisha again. 'What a beautiful girl you are! What's your name?'

As Nisha told the lady her name, a gush of pride coursed through Vaibhav's veins. This was instantly followed by a tsunami of extreme awkwardness. A compliment to the woman's son was very much in order. And it had to come out now. And it had to be effective.

'Your son is very cute too!' he pulled the boy's cheek. *Cliché. You can do better. Involve the husband. Involve the husband.* He turned to the husband, and added. 'He looks just like you.'

'No, he does not,' the man spoke for the first time. The lady stared at both men, open-mouthed.

'I think he does,' Vaibhav said. It did not matter whether he really resembled the man. Mentioning that a child resembled his father was at least a reasonable way to break deadlock and to start a conversation.

'No, he does not,' repeated the man, this time with some embarrassment. 'Because I am not his father.'

The lady had obviously shut her eyes and had now turned away from the conversation completely. Vaibhav realized the man was not even standing *with* her and the little boy; he was an inch ahead of them. *Too much sunlight, it made me bleary.*

The man raised his own folder of personal documents in the air, and smiled for the first time. He flicked one finger towards the lady and said: 'We are not together. I am Rakesh, by the way!'

The wait only got longer. Vaibhav flushed with embarrassment before remembering he had read somewhere that everyone in the world resembled someone or the other. He spent some time trying to convince himself that the boy did, after all, resemble Rakesh By The Way, even if the latter was not his father. Then he gave up on the analysis and made small talk with Nisha instead. Nearly an hour later, a security guard was spotted sauntering between the two rows, imposing discipline by wagging his finger or sometimes with a short wave of his baton. It was nearing five in the evening, and Nisha was running out of energy and patience.

'Let me go ask him what's going on.' Vaibhav handed Nisha's school bag to her and wiggled out of the queue from under one of the steel bars.

'Boss,' he tapped the guard on the shoulder. 'Our appointment was for two-thirty. It's four-thirty already.'

'I know,' replied the guard indifferently as he continued waving his baton at no one in particular.

'Why is it taking so long?'

'Tea break,' muttered the guard unhappily. 'Fifth tea break since morning. This one is an emergency tea break. Even worse.'

'Emergency?'

'Yes, they are out of Parle-G biscuits,' the guard laughed. 'They have sent the peon to get four packets. Our *saab log* can't function when hungry. Now please get back in line so that we can all do our bit to be able to go home early.'

Vaibhav spotted a water tap behind the compound wall and waited patiently for two houseflies to finish feasting on leaking water drops. He then cupped some water in his hands and drank gratefully before returning to the queue. He noticed six more irritated and angry patrons were now lined up behind where he and Nisha had been standing. He politely jostled around to make it back to his original position, when the man right behind Nisha took strong exception to his audacity.

'Boss, where do you think you are going?' demanded the man angrily. 'What are we doing in this line, swatting flies?'

That would not have been a bad idea considering how many flies were prancing around them. But Vaibhav did not offer that suggestion. 'Arre, I was already standing here. I had just stepped out to talk to that guard.'

'Stepped out once is stepped out for good,' the man poked a finger towards him. 'Move back now. End of the line.'

The lady with the little boy who did not resemble Rakesh By The Way testified. 'Let him come. He is this girl's father.' She patted Nisha on the head to provide evidence to the angry patrons.

'He might be, we don't care,' said the man before glowering at Vaibhav again. 'Did you hear me? Get back at the end of the line. Is there anyone here who does not agree with me?' He turned to the five fellows behind him, who naturally concurred with him.

Nisha, who was now tired and parched and was anyway upset with everything around her, tugged at her father's elbow. 'Papa, we can move behind.'

Vaibhav gently pushed her back to her original position and tried reasoning with the man again. 'Boss, we have been in this line since two-thirty. Let's be reasonable.'

He tried squeezing in next to Nisha when the man got hold of his collar. Nisha watched the skin of her father's neck crinkle under the pressure of the man's hand. His ears turned red as he shrugged and struggled to let go of the man's grip. She stood still and watched the show: helpless, furious, petrified, teary-eyed.

The man pushed Vaibhav as he released his collar with a jerk. 'You won't understand like this, will you?'

Large gasps escaped the audience's mouths. Nisha heard murmurs in support of and against Vaibhav. She absorbed them quietly in the hope that this would all settle soon. But Vaibhav was not willing to allow six applicants to get ahead of him by way of brute force.

With some struggle he maintained his balance and whispered in the man's ear. 'Please don't create a scene. I don't want to fight. My daughter is standing next to me.'

'And yet you don't understand,' the man was now livid. He jabbed his open palm into Vaibhav's chest and sent him crashing into the steel bars behind him. The sound of bone rattling against metal resonated through the warm evening air. With his dazed eyes, Vaibhav sensed his daughter cry out 'Papa!' as she bent forward to help him to his feet. He could not feel his own tears. But he could see, although vaguely, that she was crying. Some people were now cursing the man who had overreacted. But he stood adamant in his position. Rakesh By The Way, who had been idly watching the proceedings all along, now came running to haul him up and to tell him his shirt had got ripped at the back.

They examined the jagged protrusions on the top bar. 'Must have been one of those nasty things,' Rakesh observed.

It did not matter. It had been decided. Vaibhav moved behind to the end of the line with Nisha in tow. Moving behind came easy to him. Getting cowed down by a bully also came easy to him. He had been bullied by his former business partner, by his relatives who demanded a share in his father's property, by the likes of Samar Yadav. But this time was different, and worse. He had allowed himself to get bullied in front of his daughter. He stood behind his assailant now, in submission, even as the crowd uttered whispers of sympathy for him. The gash in his wounded back was just the size of a small crescent. But his soul felt like it had been riddled by a crater.

It was nearly dinner-time when they got home after getting her picture clicked, submitting her passport application fees, and playing dumb when the officer asked him if he would like to offer him some *malai* for smoother processing of her passport.

'Does it hurt a lot?' was the first thing Nisha asked him as they were about to finish dinner.

The question hurts more than that well-designed cut. 'No.'

'Why didn't you hit him back?' she fought back her tears.

Without waiting for his response, she walked to the kitchen, rinsed her plate and dunked it in the sink. He sat slumped in his chair, a vanquished, clueless father, well aware that she had asked a valid question that warranted a sensible answer. She went in for a shower, during which time he returned to his room, soaked a ball of cotton in Dettol and smeared it on the crescent carved on his back. The pain sent a shiver up his spine. He squealed like an infant, put his kurta back on, and went to check on Nisha. She was out of her shower and seemed to be reading a textbook with very little interest.

'About your question,' he said, pulling a chair next to her. 'I did not hit that man back because that was not the right thing to do at that time.'

'But he hit you,' she reminded him.

He bit his lower lip in acknowledgement. That shooting pain in the back now rapidly moved along his fevered head and his burning eyes. Humiliation has its gradients: one where you are humiliated and there is no one to watch what happened; the second is where your humiliation doubles up as a circus for an amused crowd; the third gradient is when your daughter whose hero you have always tried to be happens to be part of the crowd that has witnessed your humiliation. And then there is a fourth, special-class gradient where your daughter is reduced to tears as she reminds you that you were humiliated. Vaibhav had acquired platinum-class humiliation that night.

'What did you think of that man who pushed me?' he asked her gently.

'He is a bast...' she bit her tongue and checked herself.

Vaibhav looked on, stumped at her half-use of the banned word. He wondered how many more surprises she had in store for him that year. 'Please don't use such words. You are too young to use them.'

'I am sorry,' she said embarrassedly.

'In fact, no age is a good age to use that word,' he provided an add-on advice.

'I said I am sorry,' she said again. 'I meant he was not a nice man.'

'Then you have answered my question,' he said, getting up. 'Had I hit him, I would have been a "not a nice man" tonight. Do you understand? It would have left no difference between me and him.'

'Ok,' she replied, unconvinced.

'I am not saying one must be submissive,' he explained. 'But hitting someone does not always solve a problem. I could have socked him in the eye. Would that have made him a better person? Think about it. Now get back to your books and concentrate on your exams.'

She got back to her books, but could not concentrate. She could not help but recall Rupali and her scornful comments and her retaliation. Had that made Rupali a better person? Who cared – that punch she landed on the girl's eye was the only thing that had made her even slightly happy in the last couple of months. If there was merit in what her father had just told her, she could not see it just yet.

He lay in bed on his side, conscious of the skin that had softened around his wound. They were now one step closer to planning an exotic, unaffordable holiday. And he was one step further away from decoding her mysterious behaviour. He also feared the possibility that all this investment in the Australian tourism industry might not fetch him any returns if she stayed disinterested like this going forward. *Why didn't you hit him back?* He asked himself angrily before tumbling into deep sleep.

Lonely, I am so lonely

'I totally understand your concern, sir,' Rachna said for the third time. 'I am very sorry for the inconvenience.'

'Stop apologizing,' Vaibhav was fed up of trying to understand the credit card. 'I have twenty thousand points now. And you still can't get me one free ticket on the sector?'

'I am very sorry for the…'

'Can you say something new, please?' he pleaded with her. 'I am running out of patience.'

'Sir, I know I had told you twenty thousand points could get you a free ticket,' she clarified. 'But that was then. Now the flight fares have gone up further.'

His heart sank. 'So, now? I will have to pay the entire fare?'

She put him on hold and returned after a minute. 'Sir, you are our privileged customer.'

'Oh. You had me there.' He said sarcastically.

'I will discuss this matter with my manager and call you back,' she promised him.

Two hours later, she called him in an encouraging tone. 'Great news, sir! Our manager has recommended an alternate option: You can go for a part-redemption and part-purchase.

So we can offer you a discount equivalent to your credit points on your overall purchase of the round trip for two.'

'How much will it come to?' he asked without bothering to apply his mind to any more calculations.

'Sir, eighty-five thousand will be the final fare you will have to pay,' she said after checking the latest price tables online.

He gulped. But eighty-five thousand sounded a lot better than a hundred and thirty thousand. 'Alright. Book them please.'

'Sure sir,' she said. 'I will email you the confirmed tickets soon. Sir, there is an add-on family card that we are now offering…'

'No, Rachna,' he stopped her. No more credit cards for him. 'Just the tickets, please.'

At the end of her last exam, Nisha followed her annual routine of paying a courtesy visit with Vaibhav to Leena Madam's house.

'I hate this part of the year,' Leena Madam complained. She semi-lay in Vishnu's posture on the wrought iron swing in her balcony. Vaibhav and Nisha sat before her on petite stools, like submissive students. She had her guests served a glass each of *Solkadhi*.

'Why, madam?' Vaibhav asked.

She wiggled a finger in Nisha's direction. 'Because my favourite students disappear for an entire month! Leaving their Leena Madam alone.'

Nisha smiled on cue. A long, vacuous smile that she had perfected in the last three months for the sake of courtesy.

'Arre, Kulkarni saab – what was the need for this?' she brandished a packed box of sweets. 'I have told you earlier also. I teach for the love of music. It is my selfish interest.'

Vaibhav smiled at her. She was one woman Vaibhav had little difficulty conversing with, maybe because she was his mother's age. 'Madam it is a small gesture. I wanted to apologize for Nisha's irregularity in the last few months.'

Leena Madam looked bluntly at Nisha's expressionless face and shrugged. 'Fine by me. She is still my best student.'

'You are kind,' Vaibhav replied, fixing a gaze on Nisha, half-expecting her to apologize as well. She did not.

'Nisha, I must tell you one thing, though,' Leena Madam continued. 'Talent rusts away very easily. You need to polish it regularly with discipline. And discipline comes from passion. Do not let that passion die. If it were so easy for stars to be born purely of talent, every girl in this country would be Lata Mangeshkar today.'

'Yes, ma'am,' Nisha replied softly.

'I want to see you acquiring a *Vishaarad* in classical music three years from now,' she commanded.

'Yes, yes, madam,' Vaibhav nodded enthusiastically. On their way out, Vaibhav whispered to Nisha: 'What is a *Vishaarad*?'

She explained in a monotone but to his satisfaction as they drove to Miss Suzanne's.

Miss Suzanne lived in a bonsai but aesthetically decorated apartment in Bandra. There was more furniture in it than what one would imagine suited a single woman's needs. Two couches were put together in an L-formation, and a tripod in the space ahead of them. A furry rug was laid out in the centre of the living room. An array of paintings, all made by her, were pinned to various corners of the wall. They were not beautiful paintings. But she had considered them worthy of framed display, and so Vaibhav complimented them duly. There were a few antique pieces as well, such as an old gramophone that hung its head down in shame, and a brown trunk with some Indian art carvings on it. They clearly had little utility; one would think they had simply been placed as props in order to offset the lonesomeness the house otherwise seemed to wear on its sleeve.

'I love all things antique,' she commented on seeing Vaibhav admire the trunk.

'I see.' Vaibhav was awkwardly reminded of Bali's supposed observation about Miss Suzanne's soft corner for him. One thought led to another and he began wondering if she had just subtly referred to him as antique. She would not have been wrong if she had, at any rate. Then he checked himself in time when he realized it was very pompous to give in to a rumour about a woman's interest in you. Especially when you are Vaibhav Kulkarni.

'I am so glad you kept your word,' Miss Suzanne told him. 'Finally.'

'Our pleasure entirely,' said Vaibhav. 'Nisha talks so much about you all the time. She is always full of admiration for you.'

'Nisha hardly talks at all these days, doesn't she?' Miss Suzanne looked at Nisha compassionately, eliciting an answer that she did not get.

'Shall we eat?' Miss Suzanne changed the topic and guided them towards her dining table: an oval table top with three chairs and only enough room for two casseroles to squeeze themselves in its centre. The dinner was not elaborate and was consumed without much small talk.After dinner, Miss Suzanne guided Nisha towards the television room inside. 'Darling, Papa and I will have a chat. Why don't you make yourself comfortable inside?'

During better days, Nisha would have seen the funny in Miss Suzanne wanting to share a private moment with Vaibhav. But that night she chose not to react. Instead, she quietly complied and disappeared into the television room and absently flipped channels. Outside, their host served all of them Belgian chocolate ice-cream – a triple scoop for the child so she could remain distracted for a longer time in the quarantine.

'How is she doing at home?' Miss Suzanne enquired with Vaibhav once they were alone in the living room.

'You tell me, madam,' he said. 'She spends longer hours in school. And I know you have always been her mentor there. You watch her closely.'

'What I have noticed is not nice,' she said unhappily. 'I am sorry if I sound intrusive. But is it a family issue?'

Vaibhav flinched. There is no way to not sound intrusive when one asks someone about a family issue. Suzanne meant well. But the very sound of "family issues" felt like a death knell to him.

'I think I have always given her the love and attention she requires,' he said defensively.

'I have no doubt there,' she said. 'I just wonder if…Vaibhav, does she miss not having her mother around?'

Vaibhav was stunned. He had been asked the question before, but not by a pretty woman whose appealing beauty he was conscious of even when he did not make direct eye contact with her. His gaze flitted briefly towards her slender silhouette under the dimly lit room – only a large antique chandelier hanging from the centre of the ceiling, and a bulb jutting out of the mouth of a black stone panther next to the gramophone.

'I don't think so.'

He stole an opportunity to look at her one more time before turning his gaze away. She wore a red cotton skirt that reached her knees. A sash of nearly the same shade was tied around her slim waist. Her hair was tied back firmly in a ponytail. He noticed how the skin on her shins shone under the rays of the chandelier. For the briefest minute since the night he had been abandoned by Varsha, he felt he was going weak in the knees.

'I don't think she misses her mother,' he disrupted the thoughts brewing in his head.

'Do you miss your wife?' she asked.

He turned to her again. She had gotten prettier in the last minute. He wanted to tell her the truth. *I miss her every day. But I hate her more than I miss her. I do miss the presence of someone who can complete me.* 'I am used to her not being around,' he barely managed to speak.

'Loneliness is a tough beast, Vaibhav,' she was staring at her feet as she spoke. 'It hounds you even harder when it finds you trying to escape it.' Then, looking at him slowly with her caramel eyes, she said: 'I know loneliness.'

He involuntarily inhaled the scent of her hair. He had nothing to say. He was stranded somewhere between duty and desire. And in his universe, the two were not likely to intersect.

As though reading his mind, she slipped her soft palm under his. 'From my perspective, you are still a lucky man. You have Nisha. Be sure there are people lonelier than you. I sometimes wish I had a child like her.'

He trembled feverishly on feeling her skin against his. It reminded him of the time he had sat in a massage chair as part of a free sample experience in a mall. He was conscious that he was sweating under the collar, under his arms, above his moustache, but most importantly on the hand she was holding so firmly. He imagined his sweat trace its way through the lines on his palm before travelling on to hers. That feeling was not likely half as endearing as it possibly sounded.

He retracted his hand politely. 'You are very nice, madam. Nisha keeps telling me how much you care for her. I am grateful.'

He saw a glimmer of joy in her eyes. She opened her mouth to speak. He regretted cutting her off, but he had no choice. 'I am grateful there is someone who cares for her as much as I do. You asked me about loneliness, yes? I will not lie. It bites me. But I also know Nisha needs my undivided attention. It leaves me with no room to accommodate any other priority at this stage of my life.'

She replied with a calm exterior. 'Of course. You are right.'

'But I am grateful to you, madam,' he reiterated. 'Thanks for being there for her.'

'You don't need to thank me,' she shook her head with a smile.

They called for Nisha, who switched off the television and walked out towards them.

'Ready to go?' he asked her, to which she nodded.

They thanked their host, who made no attempt to hide the tears welling up in her eyes as she kissed Nisha on the forehead.

Zombie

'Welcome to Sydney!' Vaibhav read aloud from the cloth banner hanging overhead at the taxi rank outside the airport. 'Who would have thought, huh? We are in Australia!'

'Is that The Opera House?' Nisha pointed at the icon next to the banner. She held her pink travel trolley on her own, despite her father's repeated offers to tow it around for her.

'It is, indeed,' said an elderly ground official at the kerb who was guiding passengers to the next available cab. 'Are you here sight-seeing?'

'We are here to meet Rihanna,' Vaibhav said excitedly.

The official laughed. 'Aha! When you meet her, tell her I said hi.'

He motioned towards a cab that had just pulled over next to them. Vaibhav shook hands with him. 'Of course we will!'

The official blew out a puff of air in amusement. Vaibhav returned the gesture, assuming it might be a local custom. The cab drove them out of the airport on to the wide, pothole-free roads of the city's suburbs. On either side were quaint townhouses, symmetrically lined shrubs, and lush green landscapes in the space that yielded.

Nisha looked excitedly out of the window. 'It looks just like the towns described in Enid Blyton's books!'

'Who is he?' Vaibhav asked.

'She,' he was corrected. 'She was an author.'

She pulled out a camera from his bag and clicked pictures of whatever view she could lay sight on: merry cyclists, variously coloured tree leaves, and the numerous city parks. Every once in a while she turned to him and asked him if he also found the sights as enthralling as she did. He concurred each time, and beamed on seeing her smile after ages. And he felt proud he had taken what seemed to be an effective if expensive travel decision.

'Can we spot kangaroos here?' she asked the driver, pointing at a warning put up on the roadside with the silhouette of a kangaroo leaping across it.

'Not unless you are very lucky, no,' replied the driver. 'You need to visit them in the wilderness if you want to play with them.'

'Will we go visit them?' she turned to Vaibhav hopefully.

It was a tight schedule planned on a shoestring budget. He could only afford so much as the concert passes, their serviced apartment rentals and the flight fares. He did not want to give her any additional hope. 'I am not so sure. We are here for just three days. Let us see how we go.'

They checked into their service apartment, a cost-effective but comfortable arrangement in the heart of the city. The receptionist handed them brochures detailing the key attractions in and around Sydney.

'We can get you discounted tickets to most of these places,' she said cheerfully, and then asked. 'Are you attending the Rihanna concert tonight?'

'Yes, we are primarily here for the concert,' said Vaibhav.

'Have you got your passes already?'

'Yes I bought them online weeks ago,' he replied.

She twitched her lips and smiled sheepishly. 'I wish you had checked with us, Mr. Kulkarni! We could have given them to you at a thirty per cent discount had you bought them from our desk.'

He wished she had not told him that. 'My bad luck! Nothing much we can do about it now, can we? Thanks for the brochures. I might get their tickets from you tomorrow.'

'Great, have a wonderful stay,' she directed them towards the elevator before returning to her business.

They entered the apartment and dropped their bags on the floor, exhausted.

'That bed looks very soft and comfortable,' Vaibhav groaned, conducting a free fall on the mattress.

'Papa, look at the view!' she exclaimed, opening the curtains of the window. 'Do you see that building?'

She pointed at a giant skyscraper of the Westpac bank. With half-closed eyes Vaibhav looked out reluctantly at the buildings that decorated the skyline of the central business district. He looked at the posh Westpac corporate office and imagined what it would be like to work in that building. If nothing else, that workplace certainly afforded its employees a better view than the sewers outside Synergy Software that gently merged into River Mula. He tried not to imagine what salaries were offered to investment bankers in Australia. He tried not to imagine how differently life would have panned out had he dared to challenge his father's instructions and set out to pursue an elite MBA degree the way Bhandari did. Would he have ended up working in a similar skyscraper with suitably towering salaries?

He fought the urge to wonder what he would be doing at that very instant had he accepted Taneja's offer a month ago to work on that Brazilian project. Then he brushed off all those thoughts with a wave of his hand.

'Draw the curtains, please,' he crinkled his eyes tiredly.

'I can see the Darling Harbour from this side,' she leaned across the frame of the window, looking out. 'Can we go out and explore?'

'Not until you get some sleep,' he patted the other side of the bed. 'Or you are going to walk into that concert looking like a zombie.'

'I am not tired at all,' she said, excitement all over her face.

He was happy to note the excitement, but he felt like his bones had been tumble-dried in a washing machine. 'But I am. Let's sleep for a couple of hours. And then we get ready and take a walk along Darling Harbour. Done?'

Reluctantly, she lay down in bed. But sleep didn't come easy to her. She continued staring out the window for nearly an hour before slowly falling asleep. Vaibhav, on the other hand, knocked off immediately and slept like a baby. When they woke up, the alarm clock by his bedside read three-thirty in the afternoon.

'Alright Sydney! Here we come,' Vaibhav lazily stretched his arms out. 'Who is hungry?'

'I have been hungry for over an hour,' Nisha replied. 'But I haven't seen you sleep so well in a long time. I didn't feel like waking you up.'

He pulled her cheek affectionately. 'That is why I love you so much. Now let's get ready real quick and go out and eat.'

They took turns to take hurried showers and set out for a leisurely walk along Darling Harbour. They were enamoured by the view of the bay and the various restaurants and pubs that ran along its circumference. They bought two frankies from a stall and ate as they walked. They were entertained by various street performers – the statue in white paint that suddenly moved when they inched closer to him, the man who danced on a bed of knives, and the jester who mimicked everyone from Charlie Chaplin to Justin Bieber, amidst loud cheers from onlookers. Every few minutes, Vaibhav turned to his daughter and gladly noted the shift in her countenance. He saw her throaty laughter return. And just in a moment, every penny spent on that trip felt justified. He always knew he would never be able to show her the world. But he did hope he could make those three days mean the world to her.

They stood and watched the jester for an hour or more, until the crowd around them dispersed. Then they continued their walk along the promenade until they found a shaded bench outside a café.

'Someone out here should be able to help us with directions to The Opera House,' he looked around them and finally spotted a cleaner smoking a cigarette outside the café. They walked up to him and showed him their concert passes which had the address printed on them.

'The Opera House, hmm,' the cleaner pondered. 'There are various ways you could get there. You could take a taxi...'

'What's the cheapest way?' Vaibhav put forth his condition.

'The cheapest is you catch a ferry from the pier across,' the cleaner pointed in the direction of a dock less than thirty feet away. Some passengers were lined up near the barricades, waiting for the next available boat ride. 'You will need to get off at the third stop – Circular Quay, and then take a short walk to The House.'

'Wonderful,' Vaibhav thanked him. 'And we buy the tickets to the ferry from the pier?'

'Yes, you do,' he replied, and then looked at his watch, and then carefully at the passes. 'But if I were you I would skip the ferry and swim across to The Opera House right away.'

'What do you mean?' Vaibhav asked, suddenly worried.

'Your concert starts in twenty minutes, mate!' the cleaner held up his pass. 'Your ferry is going to take you a little longer than that to get there.'

Vaibhav stared at the passes in horror. The concert time was printed in very clear script: 18.00 hours. He had no time now to wonder how in the ever loving world he had read that as 8.00. He turned white with fear and looked at Nisha.

'Oh no, Papa!' she cried. 'It is 5.45 already!'

'Let's run!' he said, and they made a dash for the pier.

But there was little use, for the lady selling the tickets told them they had at least ten minutes before the next ferry embarked on its journey.

'Actually we have a concert to attend,' Vaibhav requested, desperation all over him. 'If only you could get us on the boat sooner…'

The lady shrugged. 'We stick to schedules. I am sorry. Let's just hope Rihanna is not as punctual as I have heard she is.'

Dejected, they joined the queue and waited for the giant red ferry to take its own sweet time to begin its thirty-minute journey to Circular Quay. When they finally got to their destination, it was nearing 6.25.

He held her hand and led her in a sprint to the façade of The Opera House, where they were intercepted by three security guards.

'Sir, there is a show in progress inside,' said one of them. 'We are not allowing visitors at this point.'

'Yes, yes, we are here for the same show!' Vaibhav held out his passes hopefully.

The guard shook his head. 'I am afraid you are late, sir. We cannot let you in.'

'Please adjust, no?' Vaibhav pleaded. 'It must have just started, right?'

'Yes, sir, but it is an indoor performance and the doors are closed,' he affirmed. 'There is nothing you and I can do about it now.'

'Sir, we will just sneak in quietly and take our seats,' Nisha pitched in. 'We have come from very far away.'

'Look darling,' the officer bent down to meet the girl in the eye. 'I feel your pain, alright? But we cannot disturb the performer when she is already on stage. Now don't push me on a guilt trip. I cannot help you.'

The other officer stepped forward and joined the discussion. 'Now if you could please retreat, sir, this area was meant to be cordoned off after 6.00 pm.'

A bunch of organizers with microphones stuck in their ears heard the commotion and ran up to the group. 'Alright guys, what's up?'

Vaibhav saw the organizers sporting the logo of the event management company that was managing the show. 'Are you from the organizing committee?'

'Yes. How may we help?'

'Look, sir,' Vaibhav began his pitch again. 'I have brought my daughter all the way from India only so that she can attend Rihanna's concert. She is a huge, huge fan of the star. Please let us in. I apologize we are late. We are new to this place and couldn't find our way. Just let us in this once, please?'

He turned to his daughter. 'Nisha, tell them – you know every Rihanna song at the tip of your tongue, don't you?'

The security officials shook their heads in amusement. Nisha realized this was not going to work. She pulled at her father's hand to lead him away from the organizers before the scene turned ugly.

One of the security officials spoke again. 'Sir, we have been very polite and peaceful so far. We would like to keep it that way. Will you co-operate with us, please? Will you help us stay calm and not lose our cool?'

'Of course.' Vaibhav stepped back a little. But he continued looking at The Opera House with his teary eyes.

'Good,' said the official, escorting the father and the child out of the security cordon.

Vaibhav stood behind the cordon and called out to the organizer again. 'Can we at least get a chance to meet Rihanna once the show is over?'

The organizers looked at the guards, and then nodded. 'Alright, we will let you in. She will be doing a photo-op right here on the steps at the façade. You can get some pictures then. Try and be here before nine-thirty so you can get in front of the crowd.'

'That's not what I meant,' Vaibhav said. 'We want to *meet* her. As in, my daughter wants to say hello. We will just take two minutes.'

The organizers joined the security officials in laughter this time. 'Alright, you really got us there, sir! You are a funny guy, that's all we can say. Have a good night.'

He retreated unhappily and turned to Nisha, who was now seated on a stone bench with her sad face cupped in her hands. He had made her a promise and had failed to fulfil it. He stood next to her and swayed from one foot to another, struggling to come up with an excuse in defence of his carelessness.

'These people are very stubborn,' he said finally. 'How does it matter to a star performing before a thousand fans if two of them turn up half an hour late?'

Nisha did not respond. He squatted in front of her and held her hand. 'I am sorry, Nisha. It is entirely my fault. I was so hassled with all the planning I misread the time of the concert completely.'

'We were so close,' she said softly. 'Do you think we will be able to even take a look at her properly?'

He read the angst in her eyes. There was no point thinking if they would be able to take a look at her. The plan was to meet her and there was no question of settling for the second best option.

He was not entirely convinced himself, but he thought it only fair to reassure her. 'Leave it to me. I have brought you this far. We are not going back without meeting her.'

You're givin' me such sweet nothing

They took a table at an eatery by the harbour. Every molecule of the place screamed "UNAFFORDABLE! OFF LIMITS" in Vaibhav's face. But Nisha asked him if they could eat by the harbour because the bridge looked so pretty under lights. And after the blunder he had committed by causing them to miss a concert, which by the way, meant two hundred dollars washed down the drain, fulfilling her request for an exotic dinner was the least he could do.

'I will have a chicken stro…' she pointed at an item on the menu.

'A chicken stroganoff? Sweet,' said the steward.

'Is it sweet?' she asked. 'Uh no, then, I will go for a…'

The steward laughed. 'No, I meant sweet as, um, perfect. Perfect choice. And what about you, sir?'

Vaibhav was slyly examining the price of the perfect choice on the menu. Fifty-two dollars. He looked up at the steward and shook his head. 'Nothing for me, please.'

'Why not?' Nisha asked him.

'I am too tired to want to eat,' he lied.

'Then I've got the perfect potion to refresh you,' another steward from the café came striding towards their table with a black bottle in his hand. 'Why don't you taste a free sample of our signature white wine, sir? It will soothe your senses like that!' He snapped a finger before Vaibhav's face.

Vaibhav did not need such an exotic pitch. The man had him at "a free sample". 'Yes, thank you. I wouldn't mind tasting a sample.'

A quarter of his glass was filled with the wine, and the first steward returned to get the perfect chicken stroganoff. When the food arrived, the steward holding the bottle of wine returned to their table.

'How was the wine, sir?'

Vaibhav realized he was too lost and disappointed in himself to have remembered to taste it yet. He took a large gulp. It tasted sweet and better than anything else he had ever drunk that far. It helped him forget about Rihanna. It helped him forget he had mucked up severely with the plan.

'Sweet!' Vaibhav remarked. 'As in, the perfect choice.'

'Wonderful!' exclaimed the steward. 'Shall I pour you some more, then?'

Only a fool would decline a second helping of a free sample. Filling himself up with free white wine sounded like a much better idea than ordering a fist-sized chicken breast for fifty dollars. 'I don't mind, thank you.'

He offered his glass to the steward, who filled it to the brim this time and then left the unfinished bottle on their table before walking away.

'Has he left the entire bottle for me?' Vaibhav asked doubtfully.

Nisha shrugged; she did not know. She was busy polishing off her food and seemed content with it. Just then her phone buzzed with short, staccato rings.

'Who is calling you?' he asked. 'And why have you kept your phone on international roaming? Turn it off.'

'There is no sim card in it,' she said. 'Those were my Whatsapp notifications. This place is wi-fi enabled, it seems.'

She glanced through her phone to check her messages. After a quick look she flicked it back on the table, away from her.

The phone continued buzzing. 'Who is it?' he asked her.

'Nobody.'

The nobody continued sending messages for the next five minutes before the phone went quiet. Vaibhav contently drank from his refilled glass; drinking before his daughter in Pune was uncalled for, but here he was on a holiday. All seemed well with the dinner until the sight of the unfinished bottle unsettled him. He waved at the second steward who ambled over to him in a sprightly jaunt.

'You like it?' the steward offered a fist bump. 'You want another bottle for home?'

Vaibhav returned the fist bump, but along with a firm shake of the head. He was now well past the notion that the steward had just taken pity on his tired and woebegone and defeated face and was offering him one refill after another of his best white wine, all for free.

'No, no!' Vaibhav thrust the unfinished bottle back in the steward's hands. 'Could you just take this bottle back? I am done.'

'You are done?' the steward leant back in horror. 'You are done, sir? And what about that beautiful liquid swimming in your glass, half of which you have already consumed? Are you done with that too?'

'Ok.' Vaibhav nervously returned his glass as well.

The steward smirked and waved at his colleagues frantically before turning to his two stunned guests. 'Why would you return me a bottle of wine after sampling like, let me see…' he examined the bottle, '…three-fourths of it, sir?'

Too embarrassed to say he had assumed he was still being offered samples, Vaibhav blurted, 'I…I changed my mind.'

'You changed your mind!' The steward absorbed Vaibhav's admission with dismay. He then waved the half-empty bottle at his colleagues and went running back to them like a baby whose toy had just been broken by a bully. 'He changed his mind! He changed his mind!'

Vaibhav's legs trembled like frail leaves even as Nisha stopped eating her chicken stroganoff owing to the confusion. He stared at the stewards engaged in a huddle, wondering what they were going to demand next: either he pay up for the wine, which he read was priced at a hundred and seventy dollars; or he be arrested or something, which would have repercussions far greater than the penalty of a thousand-odd dollars he would have to pay in order to get the hell out of there.

Five minutes later, the first steward returned to their table as Vaibhav stared at him with bated breath. He handed them the bill in a large mug on which was printed: SEE YOU SOON AGAIN. Vaibhav smiled in spite of himself.

'So the wine didn't pass muster, eh?' the steward winked. 'Unfortunately the poor chicken has already lost its life for your meal, so it won't be fair to let you guys just sample it.'

Vaibhav noticed the second steward offer him dirty looks from a distance. 'I am sorry, I didn't realize…'

'Don't worry about Fred,' the steward noticed the embarrassment on his face. 'He takes his wines seriously. You didn't like it, you don't pay for it. Enjoy your meal, miss.'

He bowed a little for Nisha before leaving their table. Vaibhav picked up and read the bill: fifty-two dollars. It must be a really special chicken, he concluded even as his mind conducted a speedy calculation on how they would manage the next three nights in this country with the remaining forex he had in the leather shaving kit he had been carrying protectively under his arm.

'How is the food?' he asked her.

She cringed a little; her fork sliced through the chicken breast revealing nothing but whiteness. 'It is very bland.'

He would not hear that about an expensive stroganoff. He sprayed a kilogram or such of salt on her plate. 'This might help.'

It did not. Then they added pepper, followed by tomato ketchup followed by tabasco sauce. The chicken stayed as it was. At the end of their meal they had learnt that the most expensive meals in Australia were the meats which the chefs considered exquisite enough to not tamper with garnishing. They would stick to the four-dollar rolls for the rest of their trip.

Closer to nine-thirty, they began their walk back to The Opera House. The concert seemed to have just ended when they approached the security officials; they saw groups of attendees come out through the façade in small trickles. The officials had them wait behind the barricade for a few minutes until they heard suitable instructions on their walkie-talkies.

'Alright, slip right in,' one of the officials made way for them by pushing the barricade aside. 'Stand close to the steps.

You can't climb the steps. Yes, wait right there. She should be out soon, and so should the rest of the crowd.'

'Shout out your loudest hello when she is here!' the other guard hollered.

Vaibhav and Nisha braced themselves. Within minutes, the audience had poured out of the concert hall on to the steps. The rules had changed. You could now stand on the steps. Rihanna would wave like a demi-goddess from a specially built podium at least twenty feet away from the highest step. Take it or leave it. They had no time to ask the officials what they were thinking when they asked them to wait at the bottom of the staircase.

'I can't see a thing!' Nisha cried out.

They tried nudging their way up the stairs but there were just too many people. 'We will keep trying,' he said. 'One step at a time. Hold my hand.'

For every step they would try ascending, they would be pushed two down by the delirious crowd, most of whom had also raised their cell phones up in the air in preparedness to photograph their star.

Nisha was blinded by the sea of hands floating before her eyes. 'Excuse us, please!'

She shouted a few times, but was obviously not heard. Before they could move any further, there was a loud roar that erupted from the audience, accompanied by whistles and a deafening applause.

'Is she here?' Nisha asked her father who had a relatively better view because of his height.

Through whatever space yielded between the bobbing heads and waving hands, Vaibhav saw Rihanna's silhouette appear on the podium. 'Yes, she is here.'

'Papa, I can't see anything!' she exclaimed in frustration.

'Alright, let's try this,' he hauled her up in his arms such that she faced the podium. Struggling to hold his breath, he asked her: 'Do you see her now?'

She saw Rihanna's hand. It waved elegantly at her spectators. She could also hear her say something to the crowd – something about how lovely and patronizing they had been, which meant she was certainly not talking to Nisha.

'I can't see her properly,' Nisha shouted.

He heaved her up a little more until he could put in no further effort on his unutilized muscles. 'Better now?'

She now saw Rihanna's hair. It was exactly what it looked like on television. She shouted out the star's name, waved her hand, and just for a second she thought she had caught a glimpse of her face, when she felt herself lose balance.

'Get the kiddo down, mister,' someone tapped Vaibhav's shoulder. 'There are people behind you trying to get a look.'

Fearing she could get hurt if he tried any harder, he placed Nisha back on her feet. Her lips were pursed with dissatisfaction. He knew it. The outcome was a far cry from what he had imagined. Mission Meet Rihanna was almost certainly a failure.

'Last try,' he said to himself as he led Nisha round the radius of the staircase so they could be afforded a side view of the singer. When they got to one side, they noticed the star was getting off the podium and being escorted out by her security guards through the rear entrance. He held his daughter's hand and tried running towards the rear end of the building, but they were intercepted by guards barely a few feet ahead.

'That is all, sir,' said one of them. 'Please step back. The show is over.'

'Sweet,' Vaibhav muttered. 'Sweet.'

Smile an everlasting smile

'It does look nice,' Vaibhav said, examining a demo picture of the famed "Thunderboat" on a brochure.

After a lot of goading, Nisha had chosen the Thunderboat as her recreational activity for the day. Apparently, allowing yourself to be semi-capsized in the river eight times was compensation for not getting to meet Rihanna.

'I know we could not meet her,' Vaibhav admitted for no less than the tenth time. 'But let us make the best of our last two days here.'

'I am really having a good time, Papa,' she reassured him. 'We did get to see her. Now don't feel bad about it.'

That was very lame reassurance. The disappointment on her face was as evident as it could get. You don't plan a holiday for over two months only to end up riding on Thunderboat. But for an eleven-year-old, she was reasonably graceful in the art of reconciliation.

The friendly receptionist from the previous day strolled into the buffet breakfast area to check on how her guests were doing. She saw that Nisha had made do with a glass of orange juice, while her father had stacked up on every single item from the spread. *Fill yourself up with the included breakfast package. Then go hungry the rest of the day*, was his plan for the remainder of their stay.

'How did the concert go?' she asked them after greeting them warmly.

With very sad faces they gave her an account of what had transpired.

'Oh you poor dear!' she gave Nisha a comforting hug, and then asked Vaibhav. 'So now what?'

'Now we go home,' he said in a flat tone.

'Uh-huh,' she noted. As an afterthought, she added. 'Mr. Kulkarni, could you see me at the reception when you can?'

'Of course,' he replied with a confused look.

He followed her to the bell desk, telling Nisha he would be right back. At the desk he was shown a brochure detailing Rihanna's concert schedule.

'Sorry I couldn't talk to you about it before your daughter,' she apologized. 'I wondered if I might end up putting you in a tight spot. But now that you have come here all the way, why don't you consider tailing Rihanna down to Melbourne? She performs there in four days.'

'I would if I could,' Vaibhav gave a half-smile. 'This concert was very important to us. I checked the flight fares to Melbourne last night. They will just throw my budget out of whack.'

'How about trying this instead?' she held up a car rental's contact card before his eyes. 'I can speak to them for you and manage a twenty per cent discount. And forgive me for sounding greedy, but I get a tiny commission for getting them a customer.'

'Are the chauffer services included in the rental quote?' Vaibhav asked, peering into the fine line at the bottom of the card.

'Oh no, you drive yourself,' she clarified. 'You do have a license, don't you?'

'I have an Indian driving license.'

'That works just fine,' she said. 'Do think about it and let me know. Enjoy a wonderful drive from Sydney to Melbourne. Keep the car with you during your stay there. And just drop the car off at the rental agency's branch at the airport on your way back to India. It is that easy.'

It was not as easy as she made it sound. 'I will think about it and get back to you,' he said.

The concert in Melbourne was four days later. Their flight home was two days later. He had never driven outside India before and that would be a different challenge altogether, but he would deliberate over that later. He did not have the luxury of any additional splurges. He also did not have the heart to fly Nisha back after having shown her nothing but Rihanna's right hand and her hairdo. He looked at his daughter fiddling with her glass of orange juice on the breakfast table, her head placed sideways on the table in a morose gesture. He unpacked the SIM card he had bought strictly for any urgent calls that might need to be made, and boy, was there an urgency.

The phone was answered on the sixth ring, in a very groggy voice. 'Yes?'

'Rachna, this is Vaibhav.'

'Who Vaibhav?' demanded an angry, sleepy and very masculine voice.

Vaibhav stammered. 'Oh, I am sorry. Who is this?'

'I should be asking you that question,' the voice boomed, 'since you are the one eager to speak to my wife at four in the morning.'

Vaibhav looked at his watch in shock. 'I am sorry, I am not in the country and I did not realize…'

The husband woke Rachna from her sleep. 'Who is this Vaibhav?'

Rachna woke up with a start. 'Huh? What does he want?'

She shushed her husband back to sleep and took the phone. 'Vaibhav Kulkarni? Yes, sir?'

'I am sorry,' said Vaibhav. 'Were you sleeping?'

'Sir, it is four in the morning,' Rachna stepped out of her room gingerly, ignoring her husband who had poked his head out of his blanket with curiosity. 'Can I help you with something urgent?'

'Very urgent, actually,' Vaibhav took a minute to explain the situation.

'So you now want a flight out of Melbourne? Five days later?' she confirmed.

'Yes, if you can work out my best possible options, please,' he requested her. 'I am sure your bank's tie-up with the airlines can give me a better deal than the other websites.'

She hung up, promising to call back in two hours. She called back in one. The alteration in the itinerary would add another fourteen thousand rupees to his overall cost, in addition, of course, to the car rental. This was a huge surcharge on his budget, but it was also just an additional drop in an ocean of expenses.

'Please make the changes and send me an email,' he confirmed.

With a prayer on his lips and a racing heartbeat, he returned to Nisha to tell her of the change in their plan. She resisted the idea, saying she had seen whatever bit she had to see of Rihanna and her stardom.

He heard the defeatist tone in her voice. 'Never do that. Never give up on something you have wanted to do all along, especially after getting that close. We will give it another fair shot.'

'So when do we leave for Melbourne?' she asked.

'Tomorrow morning,' he replied. 'I am going to book the car right now at the reception. It is going to be one hell of a drive, so we will need to tuck into bed early tonight.'

'Are you going to drive?' she asked, horrified. 'Papa, have you driven a car before?'

'Of course I have,' he laughed. 'I drove Joshi Uncle's jeep once from Akola to Kolhapur. You were very little then. In fact, you weren't even born then.'

'And your next drive is going to be on Australian roads?' she remarked doubtfully. 'I am not sure we should do this.'

She had a valid point. Driving without experience on the roads of a foreign country was, in the language of Synergy Software's conference rooms – an "interesting challenge". But he consciously tried to shrug off all his fears in the interest of a memorable experience for her.

'We can do everything,' he shook her up from her seat. 'If we can come this far to Australia, we can also drive in Australia. Trust me. You are going to be with me in the car. I would not touch the car if I were not sure I could drive it safely. Now get up and let's go someplace.'

She smiled at his reassurance, not only because it was very endearing but also because she could read his nervousness much that he tried covering it up with exaggerated laughter and the flapping of his hands.

'The key will be to safely drive out of the city,' he said almost to himself, every few hours for the rest of that day.

'There are too many signals, too many forked roads, and those safety cameras stare me in the face very unkindly.'

They took two tickets to Madame Tussaud's and spent half a day admiring the wax recreations of celebrities, most of whose names he would get wrong until she would either correct him off her own knowledge or would show him the corresponding label below with the correct name. He did recognize Michael Jackson's statue, though. He posed alongside the pop icon, his right hand protruded upward in emulation, his left hand on his hip, his feet in the moonwalk position that was not quite right.

'Take a picture!' he asked her.

As she held her face behind the camera to photograph his broad smile, she felt a lump in her throat. She had never seen her father that happy, that expressive. He had always been the staid, calm parent who would comfort her with a hug, take her out for meals, iron her uniform, and then quietly slip into the darkness of his room only to wake up the next morning and drop her to school. She never knew what he wanted from life. He never spoke much. He was never vocal in asking her for any reciprocation. All he had ever been vocal about was his keenness to see her smile.

'One moment,' she was distracted by a tourist who came in line of the camera. 'Pose again.'

Having made him repeat the pose, she clicked the picture, and admired it for a minute before showing it to him. Her father was never the handsomest man in the room, but he wore the most honest smile. A gush of renewed love coursed through her veins. As they descended down the stairs to view the section of the sports stars, she clutched his hand and smiled. 'I am loving this trip already!'

The same honest smile reappeared on his face. Both their jobs for the day were done. He then got her to ride the Thunderboat where he heard her scream with joy every time they were sprayed with the river water. They ate delicious burgers at Hungry Jack's, dessert at The Lindt Café, and they picked up bicycles for a dollar each and rode around Martin Place. Every time they did something new, he would look at her covertly, seeking her approval in his eyes. His gaze was not lost on her. She acknowledged it each time with a gleam in her eyes or a compliment for the city or by remarking how she had never imagined Australia would be so much fun.

Inwardly, her mind was transfixed on her father's smile when he balanced his body next to Jacko. Everything else they did that day paled in comparison.

Hello, I'm going
on the road again

'After two hundred metres, at the traffic light, turn right on to Smith Street,' Erica on the installed GPS spoke.

Vaibhav manoeuvred his first successful turn on a Sydney road and sat up straight with confidence. 'Not that difficult, eh?'

'You are sweating,' Nisha noticed a trickle run down his brow.

'Ok, don't disturb me,' he strained to hear Erica now asking him to 'bear left on Hudson Avenue in twelve meters.'

'Bear left?' he looked at the GPS, confused. 'What is a bear left?'

'Bear left on Hudson Avenue,' she repeated mechanically. He missed the turn. Dejected, she sighed. 'Recalculating.'

A few more trickles of sweat escaped his brows. It was only six in the morning and they had planned their journey with care so as to avoid the city traffic. But the few cars that plied on the roads were too fast to let him afford even the slightest margin of error.

'Ok, ok, recalculate,' he said, blowing a puff of air to calm himself. 'We are in no hurry.'

'A hundred metres ahead, at the roundabout, take the second exit on to Hume Highway,' she instructed.

He was hyperventilating now. 'I see five roads jutting out of this roundabout. Which one do I take?' He shouted, as though Erica were tuned to paying attention to his cries.

'Where is the exit?' he cried out again. 'I don't see any exit signs.'

'Take the second exit on to Hume...recalculating,' she sighed again, and he sharply took a complete turn along the roundabout.

A few horns were angrily blared. A few nasty stares were directed at him. He managed to pull over next to a gas station and ask around how a second exit from a roundabout was meant to be taken. The station manager, a friendly avuncular Indian, stepped out of his store to give him a few driving tips.

'You can't just take the car out here just like that, baba,' he said, shaking his head like a mound of jelly. 'You must know the rules. These people are very strict. I got my license confiscated once. Look – there are five roads at the roundabout. So just count from the leftmost road no? One, two, three, four, five. The second road is the second exit.'

He offered a few more free tips on speed limits, lane maintenance, and most importantly, 'Don't honk just because your car has a horn. They get very upset about it. Driving was so much more fun back in Delhi, I tell you.'

With all driving lessons in place, they resumed their journey and hit Hume Highway just at dawn. The speed limit was set at a hundred and ten an hour. They cruised along the freeway, taking in the panoramic view of the sun-glazed hills, the occasional river or rivulet, and cattle that took to actual meadows and not to the roads like they did back home.

'This drive is so much better than just exploring Sydney!' Nisha said, rolling her window down and letting her hair loose.

'Music?' he asked her.

She plugged her Just A Phone to the auxiliary jack in the car's music system. They sang along, ate strawberries they had handpicked from a farm en route, and felt the wind tickle their cheeks as they sped along. He watched the winding road he was leaving behind him; every culvert and every bend grew tinier before vanishing out of sight. He absorbed the splendour of nature all around him, and in that moment all his unaccomplished dreams ceased to haunt him. His own existence felt so miniscule before the magnificence of what he saw around him that he had no more bandwidth to hold a grudge against what life had dealt out to him.

As they crossed the Canberra outback around three hours later, they began hunting for a breakfast stopover.

'I just saw a McDonald's signboard a minute ago,' she said. 'Four kilometres ahead.'

They took the exit to McDonald's; he stretched in the parking lot as she went in to consider options for a light breakfast.

He joined her inside a minute later and noticed loaves of banana bread at the McCafe counter. 'I think I am sorted, I will have one of those.'

She ordered a burger meal and requested an English breakfast tea instead of her soft drink. She handed the tea to her father as they settled on the table. 'You must miss your morning tea.'

'I really do,' he drank up in three quick gulps. 'It tastes odd, though. No masala.'

Just then, they thought they had heard someone sniffle. The café was fairly empty, and they were quick to spot the source: a middle-aged man, maybe older than Vaibhav by a handful of years, sat sobbing in his chair.

'Is he hungry?' she asked her father sympathetically.

Vaibhav laced his banana bread with butter and sank his teeth into it. 'I don't know about him. But I am.' Noting that the man's sobs were bothering her significantly, he stood up from his seat. 'Alright, let us check.'

They stepped closer to the man. 'Is everything ok?' Vaibhav asked.

'I missed my bus,' the man wept. He looked up at them with his emerald green eyes. His blond hair was ruffled up in distress. 'I was on my way to my son's graduation ceremony and the bus had halted here. I went for a leak, came back and saw it was gone. Now there is no way on earth I can make it to the university, and I don't know how to get home.'

'Pretty important, that graduation ceremony, right?' he offered.

'Of course,' the man replied, dabbing his tears. 'I am all he has.'

He had Vaibhav at 'I am all he has'. Vaibhav knew the 'I am all he has' syndrome very well. He felt a short-lived surge of brotherly love towards the stranger. 'I feel for you.'

'We can drop you if you like,' Nisha said suddenly. 'My father has a car.'

'Really?' the man looked up hopefully. 'Where are you guys going?'

'Melbourne,' she replied without blinking.

'That will be so great!' he grunted a little to stop his nose from flowing. 'I need to get off near Albury. I will then take the nearest bus from the freeway.'

Vaibhav looked at Nisha sharply. 'Please excuse us,' he said to the stranger and took Nisha aside. 'We don't offer lifts to strangers. Never.'

'But Papa,' she pleaded. 'He needs help. It will make him so happy.'

After some bickering, they returned to the man and asked him to stop crying and to get inside the car instead. He introduced himself as Josh, a divorced father of one. Vaibhav introduced himself as Vaibhav and a father of one and skipped details of his marital status. Over the next few hours that they drove, the three hit it on like they were best friends.

But only until Vaibhav felt some cold piece of metal brush against the nape of his neck. 'What is that?'

He tried feeling the back of his neck and ended up holding the handle of a glistening knife. 'What the hell is...'

'Shh, quiet,' Josh, the father of one, spoke in a menacing tone. 'Keep driving till I tell you to.'

Vaibhav and Nisha looked through the rear view mirror in horror. Josh had looked a lot helpless and tired back at McCafe. Now his jacket was undone and tied around his waist. And the forearm that held the knife against Vaibhav's neck was approximately as thick as the trunk of the only peepal tree that grew in the compound of Savant Co-operative Housing Society. Nisha knew it already – her lanky father stood no chance against him. She noticed patches of sweat under his armpits, and little beads forming on his moustache, just like they did when he was nervous.

'We can talk,' Vaibhav spoke after five minutes.

'Yeah, I don't mind,' Josh said, his hand still holding the knife against his driver's neck. 'I never mind a nice chat.'

'No, I mean we can talk about why you are holding that knife,' Vaibhav emphasized.

'You will know soon enough,' Josh replied, 'though if I were you I would have known by now.'

Minutes later he asked Vaibhav to pull over at a designated rest area, which was an isolated patch of land with nothing but a small bench and two squirrels watching the commotion.

'Get out of the car, you two,' Josh demanded, stepping out. 'And give me your wallets.'

'I don't keep a wallet,' Nisha replied, her hands raised in the air.

He flicked an outstretched palm towards Vaibhav, who quietly obliged by placing the wallet in his adversary's hand: limited damage, about fifty dollars in cash, and a credit card that could be immediately blocked.

'Take your license,' Josh kindly produced Vaibhav's driving license and threw it towards him.

'Thanks,' said Vaibhav, picking it up. 'Can we leave now?'

'Not so soon,' Josh checked the car boot, but was disappointed to find very modest apparel in their bags. He then checked the glove box, and found Vaibhav's leather shaving kit snuck in there.

Vaibhav ran behind Josh and tried snatching his possession back.

'Papa, careful!' Nisha shouted, but her father was already lunging for Josh's throat.

'Leave that, it is just a shaving kit,' Vaibhav struggled.

'Good, my beard has been very itchy lately, I need a shave right now,' Josh smirked, pushing Vaibhav to the ground.

The incident outside the passport office flashed before Nisha's welled up eyes. She saw her father, once again bruised and vanquished, sprawled on the floor as he watched the thug pull out the fat wad of forex which he had preserved with all his care that far.

'Don't take that, please,' Vaibhav first begged of him, and then gave him an eyeful. 'Listen, Josh. That is my hard earned money. Please let that go. I have given you my wallet.'

'I have worked hard for this too,' grinned Josh, waving the wad at his victim.

Nisha came charging at Josh in a fit of rage. He was not prepared for it. 'Step back!' he screamed at her.

But she ran into him, crashing her head into his belly. 'Give my father's money back. *Now!*'

Furious, Josh held her by her hair and knocked her head against the side door of their car. Vaibhav sprang up to his feet on seeing his daughter cry out in pain. What happened next was far beyond Nisha's wildest imagination. Barely having recovered from the shock of her head hitting metal, she saw her father charge like a beast at Josh. He first landed a slap on the man's scraggly face, forcing him to drop the knife to the floor. He then kicked the knife away and took Josh by the collar, punching him alternately in his stomach and in his jaws.

'How dare you touch her!' Vaibhav bellowed loudly each time his fist made contact with the man's skin. 'How dare you! No one hits my daughter, do you hear me?'

Nisha ran around the semi-circular rest area to look for help, but there was not a soul in sight. She looked back to find the men now engaged in a wrestling bout on the floor, hitting each other relentlessly. She ran up further and finally found a family picnicking at the far end of the patch.

'I need your help!' she screamed, tears and dust smeared on her face. 'Someone is harming my father!'

Without much ado the family of five ran to the spot where Nisha had left Vaibhav, who was now belting Josh with the sole of his shoe. The shaving kit was still firmly in Josh's hand as he put in every effort to combat Vaibhav with the occasional kick. But Vaibhav, half his adversary's size, had overpowered him and was raining down on him like a hot-blooded warrior.

'Dare you try and take my money!' he slapped Josh one more time. 'And dare you touch my girl again!'

By the time Nisha and the picnickers reached the men, Vaibhav had retrieved his shaving kit and Josh had escaped his clutch, hobbled out of sight and slinked away on to the other side of the freeway.

The father of the family learnt about their grand gesture of offering a stranger a lift on the highway, and burst into laughter. 'Never do that again!' Turning to Nisha, he said, 'Though from what we saw here, it was your brave father harming that crook, and not the other way round.'

Vaibhav and she looked at each other, smiling and sighing in relief. They were both safe and with each other. Josh the father of one or otherwise, had made off with the wallet and the fifty-dollar note in it: minimal harm caused. The forex and the precious shaving kit were once again under Vaibhav's arm.

'We have a first aid box in our car,' the mother in the family said, observing a cut on Vaibhav's forearm. 'You might want to use some.'

Vaibhav examined Nisha reactively: all was ok. After some hesitation he offered their first aid; then they thanked the family and were on the road once again.

'Are you sure you are fine?' he asked her again, looking at her frightened face next to him.

'I am fine,' she said. 'What about you?'

'I am fine if you are,' he grinned. 'Quite an adventure.'

'Why did you hit him?' she asked suddenly. 'I mean, why did you hit this man and not hit that other guy at the passport office? They were both wrong.'

They had driven into Victoria. The brown landscapes had made way for much greener pastures, and the sun had dimmed a little. The air grew chillier. Vaibhav turned on the heater and the headlights of the car.

'It was a different day and time then,' he replied. 'I didn't care about what happened at the passport office, because that man had not hit you. Today was different. This guy hit you, and I did not like that.'

She struggled to find her voice. 'Yes, Papa.'

He winked. 'Like I have mentioned before, one's power is meant to be used only in defence of one's loved ones, not in display of brute force. If someone tries to harm your family or tries robbing you of your possessions, you are in the right to give him a punch or two.'

'I was very scared when I saw that knife in his hand,' she admitted.

'You never need to be scared,' he looked at her softly. 'You are a brave girl. Brave people have no reason to be scared.'

She turned away from him and stared out of the window contemplatively. She could not have concealed her feelings forever, but she did not mean for them to be revealed during the holiday either. But this was as good a time as any other, she decided.

'Papa, I have to talk to you about something.'

'Yes?'

'I want to tell you what happened on the night of my birthday.'

That's how superheroes learn to fly

They drove into Melbourne's central business district shortly before dinner. The city lights had come on. They could see the towering Eureka skydeck at the horizon as they slowed down once again to understand which convoluted lanes Erica was directing them through. But he was not with Erica or her instructions, much less with the city's lit skyline. He also did not see the significance of the mega banner of Rihanna outside the Rod Laver Arena they had just driven past. He only wanted to get to their motel and access the internet, because the email Nisha had mentioned to him was so dated he remembered nothing about it.

'I chanced upon an email Mummy had written to you long ago,' she had told him in the car almost an hour earlier before bursting into tears.

'What email?' he had asked her.

She could not contain herself any more. 'I am the reason Mummy and you are not together. I have read everything.'

She briefly told him about the email. It was something about how he had run down her blockbuster plans for life with his mediocrity. But then there was something more too – something that an eleven-year-old should not have had to read, not at least on her birthday.

'Hold on,' Vaibhav had then asked her. 'You said it was written a long time ago. Why and how in God's name did you read an email written from her a long time ago?'

How she had chanced upon it was a long, unimportant story. Facebook had shown her the profile of a certain Varsha Jadhav under 'People You May Know'.

Hell yeah, I might know her. I think she used to be my mother, and she had ended up accessing the newly created profile of this lady whom she resembled a great deal. Varsha's email address was mentioned on the page. Vaibhav's Gmail account was also open on another browser. A random search of the email address on his account had led her to this email. And then ugly skeletons had tumbled out of the cupboard. Curiosity not just kills cats, it also does away with one's peace of mind.

What was really important was that Varsha's email debunked Vaibhav's vague 'Circumstances and unaligned destiny' theory he had always provided to Nisha when she asked him about her mother's whereabouts. The email, written possibly in one of the woman's angriest moments, squarely blamed him for their decision of having a baby when they both knew they were not mentally and financially ready for the big step.

...And I never wanted the baby. You said she would bring us joy. But she only brought us more liabilities. Yes, I ran away from her and I ran away from you. That is what suited me best. And you can make me the villain here all you want, but I can promise you it is only a matter of time before you also realize it was all a big mistake...

He stood up from the internet kiosk next to the motel's reception and waited for the elevator. Varsha had challenged the longevity of his love for Nisha, who was eleven already. He had proved his wife wrong, although he had never felt the need to. But he did feel the need that night to tell his daughter that he never did and would never think of her as a mistake. He would tell her that she was the only thing in the universe that gave him reason to keep going, that she was the reward for whatever good he may have ever done in life, and that despite telling her all of this, he might fail in telling her what she really meant to him.

The door of the elevator opened. He entered their room and saw Nisha slouched against the headboard of the bed. The television was on, but she was staring at the foot of the bed. His answers were all ready in his head. But when he reached her, he only so much as managed to collapse in her arms and weep.

Hugging her tight, he whispered, 'You should have talked to me about this long ago.'

It took a while before any of them could speak further. She spoke finally. 'I knew you would be hurt if I talked to you about it.'

'Tell me, though,' he held her face in his hands. 'Don't I love you enough? I think that makes up for everything. I never thought you missed her all these years.'

'I never did,' she said. 'But you always told me she loved me too.'

Oh no, the perils of seemingly harmless twisted truths. Yes, so he had said this to her a few times. And it turned out that was not entirely true.

'So what?' he argued. 'We get some, we lose some. I don't want you to believe one word of whatever was written in there.

I have always loved you and will continue to. This is the only truth.'

He pondered over the repercussions this email had on the little girl's mind. 'Had we discussed this earlier, you would not have faced all those problems in school. Everything is so clear now.'

She countered his conclusion. 'I don't think it was that big. I only told you about it because I felt like sharing it with you. I had almost forgotten about it two days later.'

'Then why did you stay so distracted at school and at your music classes?'

'I was upset for a day or two,' she said. 'And then I started getting pulled up by the teachers, which made me even more miserable. And then I got into a few fights. I was not able to concentrate on anything.'

'But it all started with that email,' he insisted.

She shrugged. 'I also got a lot of bad dreams those days. They would wake me up in the middle of the night.'

'Dreams of what kind?'

'That you and I are together in a train,' she recalled. 'And then you get off at a platform to buy us soda. And the train moves. And you don't get back on to it. I tap the window of the train thinking you have forgotten to board the train, but then I see you walking out of the station. And then the train is on its way ahead, and I am all alone in it, wondering what to do.'

He roared with laughter in an attempt to diffuse the tension. 'You should have pulled the chain, silly!'

Seeing she was not convinced by humour, he told her a story of when he was roughly her age. 'I was by my father's bedside, pressing his feet as a matter of nightly ritual. I don't remember what had come over me those days. But every night as I would return to bed after watching him drift into sleep, I would stand for a while by his side, observing his chest worriedly. Then in the dark of the room when I would see his chest heave a little with his breathing, I would be assured that all was right with the world, and I would happily go to bed. But one night I was so consumed by my excessive worries of my parents' wellbeing that I started crying softly while I was pressing his feet. And he woke up startled, because I used to grunt like a pig when I used to cry.'

'Like this?' she grunted in demonstration.

'Louder. That was just a bleat of a lamb.'

'So did you tell him why you were crying?'

'I did,' he nodded. 'And I expected him to laugh at my stupidity, for my fear of the unknown and the distant. But to my surprise, he told me it was completely normal for such thoughts to come to a child's mind. When you love someone, you care so much for him that you tend to drive yourself crazy with worry, he said. But he also told me it was pointless to cry about such things.'

'Yes, because one must always be happy,' she pre-empted. 'And be grateful for what we have got in the present.'

'Of course,' he said. 'But also because the future is inevitable. You cannot run away from it.'

'As in?'

He smiled. 'You know what I mean. I don't want us to discuss details of the future and its inevitability. I only want to tell you that it is not wise to worry about loneliness. One must learn how to combat it instead. I learnt it a long time ago. And I want you to learn it too. I want you to grow up to be a brave, independent woman whom people look up to for her courage and her grit.'

Reclining against her pillow, she said. 'I don't get those bad dreams now.'

'Good,' he replied, looking at his watch. 'But you must get some good sleep. It has been a very long day.'

She slipped under her blanket and turned her head to the other side. Once the lights were out and she knew he was asleep, she pulled out her phone and went through the string of messages Bali had sent her on Whatsapp over the last few days.

Nisha, I tried calling you after exams. Are you out of town? Please call me. – Bali.

Hey, I wanted to say sorry for whatever happened. Really need to talk. Where are you?

And then, the next day:

Look, I know you are reading my messages. I can see the blue ticks against every message. Why can't you reply?

It's not like I am the only one who needs to say sorry. You have acted weirdly in the last few months too, by the way. But I am willing to forget everything of the past.

Ok, I am sorry. Just forget what I wrote. I am sorry for hurting you. Call me back. Let's be friends again.

And then, the same evening, shortly before they arrived in Melbourne:

I am leaving for Mauritius with my parents tomorrow. Will be back in a few days. I wish we would never have fought. I have been upset about it all this time and it has spoiled my vacation.

Looks like you don't want to talk to me. If you change your mind let me know. You are my best friend, and I don't want us to fight again.

She lay in bed wondering what to do. The bitterness from the last few months had receded and was making way for a new beginning: a dream vacation, a chance to meet her role model, a reassurance that she was never alone. She had little reason to continue being grumpy.

Hi Bali! You didn't need to be so dramatic yaar. Of course we are best friends. I am in Melbourne with Papa. I will meet you once I am back. Have a good time in Mauritius, and tell me if I can get you something from here.

She fell asleep, and was woken up shortly by another buzz:

Australia!!!! Wow!
Ok, can you get me a Cricket Australia jersey? I will pay you for it.

Hips don't lie

'Nisha, wake up!'

'Up, up, up!' He shook her by the shoulder again till she brought her groggy face from under the warmth of her blanket.

She looked out of the window; the sun was not out yet. 'What happened?'

He wore his shoes as he spoke. 'Go freshen up. Quick. We have ten minutes.'

'Where are we going?' she asked sleepily. 'It is not even morning yet.'

'It is six. The sun doesn't rise here until seven,' he said, pushing her towards the bathroom door. 'Now don't ask any more questions. We will talk on our way. I will be waiting for you at the reception. Make it fast.'

In ten minutes she joined him in the lobby, her hair dishevelled and her eyes still droopy. 'I have not even taken a bath,' she said.

'It is not necessary,' he said. 'Come on.'

He walked her to the main street from where they boarded the next available tram. As would be expected of a city that early in the morning, the roads, much like the tram, were barely occupied.

'Where are we going?' she asked again.

'To The Hyatt,' he replied. 'To meet Rihanna. I just learnt from our bell desk this morning. That is where she is put up before her show tomorrow.'

'So are we not going to the concert?' she asked with disappointment.

'We will,' he said. 'But I learnt one lesson from the Sydney experience: we can't hope to speak to her at the concert. There is too much crowd and chaos.'

'And you think we will be able to meet her at this hotel?'

'Of course,' he said. 'She won't be surrounded by lunatic fans trying to throng her. She will have time for us.'

'Papa!' she laughed. '*We* are the lunatic fans who will be trying to throng her!'

'Yes, but in a dignified way,' he raised a finger to make his point.

They got off at stop 101 right outside The Grand Hyatt. They rode the escalator up to the lobby and took a table for two at the breakfast café.

'Good morning, guys,' a steward came forward and handed them a menu card.

'Good morning,' Vaibhav returned the greeting before asking: 'Is Rihanna here?'

'No, she is not on the menu unfortunately,' said the steward and then laughed alone.

Vaibhav did not understand the joke, but he laughed in ample measure just in case that motivated the steward to help him get to Rihanna.

'She is staying with us, yes,' he said later.

'Do you know if she comes down here for her meals?' Vaibhav asked hesitantly. 'I am sure she is a very private person, so I was just wondering.'

'Nobody is too private for a good leisurely breakfast,' the steward said. 'I know she was down here yesterday morning.'

'Wonderful,' Vaibhav said. 'Around the same time as right now?'

'A little later,' he replied. 'Why don't you get yourselves something to eat before she is here? You don't want to go to her with your stomachs rumbling like empty barrels.'

Vaibhav handed Nisha the menu card. She was tempted by the description of their croissants. But then she saw the Indian Masala tea on their menu. Knowing him well to choose only between her food and his tea, she returned the menu to him.

'I can't eat anything that early in the morning.'

'Are you sure?' he asked her.

'Yes.'

He signalled to the steward and asked for – yes – an Indian Masala tea. Nisha smiled at her presence of mind. The tea arrived. He drank it leisurely, looking around the lobby every now and then. Nearly an hour later, two men in black clothes arrived at the café and whispered something to the restaurant manager, who motioned towards a table in a corner of the room. The men in black nodded tersely and walked back in the direction of the elevator. Vaibhav recognized one of the younger men as one of the organizers from The Opera House who had found it funny that they had requested a private meeting with Rihanna. He saw him now, standing with the other organizer, dialling a number and looking heavenward as he placed the phone to his ear.

Presently a commotion was sensed in the lobby area near the elevators. A shuffling of many feet was heard – a few whispers and some formal laughter that accompanied them. The staff at the reception looked excited and waved in the direction of the elevators. A few guests from the hotel, mere mortals against their object of interest, had stopped in their tracks and were looking in that direction, whispering to each other excitedly.

And then she emerged: dressed in track pants and a jumper, her purple hair pulled back by a hair band, and glares so large they covered most of her face. She walked fast, and the battalion of two security personnel, her manager, and the two organizers struggled to keep pace with her even as the restaurant manager guided her to the table reserved for her. She greeted everyone who crossed her path with a polite but short nod. No eye contact, or no Gucci Glares Contact for that matter.

'Rihanna Madam!' Vaibhav stood up from his seat and waved to catch her attention.

Nobody turned in his direction. But she offered him the same polite-but-short nod as she went on to sit at her table.

'She nodded!' He tapped Nisha fervently on the shoulder. 'Did you see that, Nisha? She acknowledged my shout-out!'

Nisha did not respond. She was in her chair, her body turned away from Vaibhav, in Rihanna's direction. With her chin placed on the back of her chair, she stared in amazement at the woman whom she had admired, idolized, and – who would have thought – hoped to meet one day. That woman now sat twenty feet away with her back towards her, still unaware of the existence of arguably her biggest fan ever.

'Get up,' Vaibhav prodded her. 'This is the only time we have.'

'I can't,' Nisha shook her head. 'I don't want to.'

'Oh, come on now,' he said irritably. 'I haven't brought you here all the way from India only to hear this. Haven't you always wanted to meet her?'

She turned to him and whispered. 'Papa, look at her. She is busy talking to her manager and to the organizers. They don't look like they will encourage us at all.'

'Why give up without even trying?' he cajoled her. 'Especially after coming this close?'

He placed his palms a few feet apart in demonstration. '*This close.* Come on.'

He could not admit this before Nisha, but he was certainly more nervous than her. He was hardly a fan of Rihanna's, in fact he didn't know a single song from her discography. But he was standing here at the threshold of his daughter's biggest dream that far. And over time, he had come to own this dream too. He had committed many an irreversible mistake and had nearly made peace with whatever repercussions he had had to face owing to his decisions. But this time, he could not afford to go wrong. Because this was his singular chance to become his daughter's hero.

He held her hand and led her to the table where Rihanna was seated, eating something very elementary in calorific value, like a bland omelette – possibly the reason these celebrities never seemed to age beyond twenty. Her manager was discussing something of utmost importance – possibly the remainder of her concert and her schedules – and the organizers were pitching in with an affirmation or a point here and there. The security personnel were hovering around a few feet away from their table, but were close enough to ward off an eager man and his daughter closing in on the celebrity they were assigned to guard.

'Hello, Rihanna madam!' Vaibhav called out once again from behind her.

She did not turn back to look at him; instead, she merely craned her neck around thirty degrees to her left. *That is all the attention you get – take it or leave it.*

Vaibhav bent down and whispered in Nisha's ear. *'Asa waattay ki tichi maan lachakli aahe.' Looks like she has sprained her neck.*

Nisha stepped behind him, gazing at the star's quarter-turned neck in amazement. He tried pulling her out from behind him, but she held on tightly to her father's shirt in fearful protest. The security personnel had stepped forward, wondering if this was an unsolicited interruption they needed to take action against.

'Yes?' Rihanna's manager spoke finally.

'We just wanted…' Vaibhav began.

'Wait,' the manager held up a hand. 'Are you the hotel staff?'

'No.'

'Then we are sorry, we cannot talk,' the manager cut him off curtly. 'Please excuse us, sir.'

'Just two minutes,' Vaibhav held up two fingers in a gesture of request. 'My daughter just wants to say hello.'

'Hello,' Rihanna spoke so softly Nisha could not have heard her even if she had pressed a cheek against hers. That neck was still craned at thirty degrees, and whatever bit of the face was visible to her audience looked in want of patience.

'Ok, got that?' the manager asked, visibly irritated. 'She said hello. Now please. This is a private conversation.'

The security personnel politely held Vaibhav by the elbow and tried leading him away. But the man had now gathered far more courage than he had while dealing with Hasmukh at The Royal Club a few months earlier.

'Please, Madam,' he said. 'Two minutes is all we need. She is a huge fan of yours, and she sings beautifully, just like you.'

One of the organizers in black stood up. 'I remember you. We met a few days ago. Had I not told you we are not allowing private meetings with Rihanna?'

'Maybe, but I still want to hear it from Madam,' he insisted. 'Madam, can you talk to my daughter for two minutes? Nisha?' He forced Nisha to come out of hiding. She did so, but her fist still tightly clenched her father's sleeve. 'Nisha, sing a song for Rihanna madam.' Looking at Rihanna's neck again, he said, 'Madam, she listens to your song – *Hips Don't Lie*– all day. You will love her voice.'

The organizers and the manager broke into a giggle. 'Alright, that is so wonderful. But *Hips Don't Lie* was sung by Shakira. You might want to go meet her.'

Vaibhav saw Rihanna's lips twitch with irritation. 'Oh no,' he said. 'Sorry. Nisha, sing any song you like.'

'Sir, please, this way,' the security personnel tried whisking him away again. But Vaibhav stood his ground.

'I am just asking for two minutes,' Vaibhav protested. 'We would have been done by now had you just allowed us to speak to Madam peacefully.'

That was it. Rihanna stood up, slamming her serviette on the table and walking away. They had still managed to see only her neck and a small percentage of her face. The organizers and the manager and the security ran after her. Vaibhav ran after all of them.

'Papa, please, stop,' Nisha pulled him back, desperately. 'They are not going to listen.'

But Vaibhav closed in on their heels. 'One minute, Madam, please.'

The manager stopped in his tracks and turned menacingly to Vaibhav. 'Sir, you are crossing the line now. You have made her very upset. She did not even have her breakfast. Do you see what you have done? Now, we are going to have to call the hotel staff and have you evicted if you don't step back.'

As if on cue, the floor in-charge of the hotel appeared from nowhere and asked the manager if something was the matter.

The manager pointed at Vaibhav. 'Are this man and his daughter guests at your hotel? I think we need your intervention.'

Vaibhav craned his neck over the manager's shoulder. 'Sorry, Madam. Really sorry. Please finish your omelette.'

The floor in-charge looked at Vaibhav sympathetically. 'Are you staying with us, sir? Can we help you?'

'Not any more, I am afraid,' Vaibhav noted sadly.

Rihanna had stormed out of the scene and into the elevator, and was back in her presidential suite in a jiffy, leaving her unannounced visitors from India high and dry once again. Her manager nodded triumphantly at them and disappeared into the elevator as well.

The floor in-charge led them back to their coffee table. 'I understand your pain. Even I haven't managed to meet her yet. Please have a seat, sir. What can we get you?'

'I had a cup of tea,' Vaibhav replied. 'Nisha, do you want something?'

She shook her head. He turned to the floor in-charge and said they would just like to pay for the tea and leave. Their job here was done, though not quite. On their way down the escalator and on to the street, he asked Nisha why she kept hiding behind him instead of standing straight and having a direct conversation with the one person she had yearned to meet for so long.

'It would have made so much difference,' he said, slightly irritated. 'Had you sung a song for her, she would have felt happy and would have talked to you. Why were you hiding behind me?'

They were out on the street now, standing next to the open air podium of the hotel. 'I brought you all the way till here. This was one step you should have taken on your own.'

'We tried meeting her twice, Papa,' she said. 'I don't want to try a third time, please. I didn't like how those people spoke to you.'

'And I didn't like how you *did not* speak to her,' he said. 'Anyway, tomorrow we attend her concert and then leave for India the next day. This was all the chance we had.'

'Sorry for not having spoken to her,' she said. 'I was just too scared of being brushed away by her.'

He turned behind. He could see the edges of the swimming pool located on the podium of the hotel. He could hear the fascinating sound of someone flapping hands in its water.

He turned to her for a second before looking behind his shoulder again. 'Your failures can never weigh as much as the burden of your regrets.'

I came along, I wrote
a song for you

They returned to the hotel and took turns to shower and to get dressed for the day. He brought the car out on the main street and she sat next to him silently, without asking questions. She knew she had disappointed him; she did not want to question the remaining plans he had drawn out for the last two days of their vacation.

He drove her to the Phillip Island Wildlife Park, where she leaped into his arms with joy on seeing at least fifty large kangaroos hopping around in the meadows of the sanctuary. There were the occasional dingoes and the emus too, but she gave them a pass and ran herself amok amidst the kangaroos. The keeper at the sanctuary handed them a packet each of kangaroo food that would help the animals get friendlier with them in due course.

'For two dollars each.'

'Just one, please,' Vaibhav offered him two dollars and took a packet. 'We will share.'

He sat on a mound, watching her chase the beasts till they gave up on the idea of running away, and bowed before her for their feeds instead. She stretched her palm out and let them lick it clean of all the food she had put out for them. He got up and took a picture of her hugging the hugest of them. The keeper at the sanctuary had named him Gargantua, as they read on the locket around his neck. Then they took to the boardwalk and spotted koalas perched on branches of a number of eucalyptus trees. Most of them were asleep; the few that were awake were too lazy to protest when she leaned close to their branches to pose for a picture.

'The kangaroos were much more fun than the koalas,' she gave her verdict as they sat in their car on their way back to the city.

'Maybe because the kangaroos made you work harder to be able to get to them,' he suggested. 'Maybe that only means we value the greatest experiences in life when we struggle and fight to get them.'

She looked at him understandingly. 'I am sorry. I should have spoken to Rihanna. I should have at least tried. We can try again tomorrow, right?'

'At the concert? That will not be easy. You know what happened at The Opera House,' he reminded her.

'We can still try.'

'Ok.'

'Ok what?'

'Ok that it is nice to hear that you would still like to try,' he elaborated. 'But I will not help you this time. You try speaking to her yourself if you can.'

'Why won't you help me?' she asked.

'Because it is your fight and not mine,' he said. 'And I want to watch you fight it all by yourself.'

'Fight?'

'This fight against your fear,' he explained. 'The fear of being brushed away by her – once again.'

'I have no fear now,' she said.

'I am happy to hear that.'

'Let us reach the Rod Laver Arena before time tomorrow,' she said. 'I will approach Rihanna myself this time.'

'I don't know what you are thinking, but just make sure you don't get us into any kind of trouble,' he cautioned her. 'There will be security all around her.'

'I will be careful.'

When they returned to the hotel that night, she asked him to return to the room; she had a little something she needed the internet for and would be in bed in good time. He did not resist. Exhausted, he retired to the room and fell instantly into deep sleep. The next morning he woke up to find himself alone in the room. He checked the bathroom; she wasn't there. He was just about to call the reception to check if they had seen her, when she swiped the card key into the door and stepped in.

'Where were you?' he asked.

'I have been so excited I could hardly sleep,' she smiled. 'I woke up really early in the morning and so I thought I'd rather take a walk along the street until you were up.'

'I am excited too,' he said, holding up the passes to the concert. 'But let's not get late today!'

They arrived at the gates of the Rod Laver Arena that evening prior to the stipulated time of the concert. The queues of spectators had just begun to form outside the entrance to each gate of the stadium. They got into their designated queue and made their way inside the arena and to the front segment of the audience. The spectators were pouring into the rows of chairs in hundreds, and the excitement inside the stadium was rising by the minute. Posters of Rihanna were being brandished by thousands of excited fans. Groups of families and friends were belting out her numbers in harmony as perfect as they could muster in that frenzied atmosphere. When the emcee got on the stage to welcome the audience and to make some terrible jokes, Nisha looked around and saw the stadium was packed to the brim with at least fifteen thousand fans who were now demanding to see what they were here to see.

'This is a dream come true!' she grinned from ear to ear, much to Vaibhav's delight. 'It is even better than I had imagined it to be!'

'I can't hear you very well,' Vaibhav screamed into her ear. 'But it looks like fun, huh? And don't worry about not getting to meet her. Let's enjoy what we have got. Such opportunities come once in a lifetime.'

'Seats 18B and 18C?' asked a voice.

Vaibhav turned to his left and saw a young volunteer inspecting the occupied seats and tallying them against some records showing on his handheld device.

'Yes.' Vaibhav replied.

'Vaibhav…' and then with some difficulty and with a severely accented pronunciation, 'Kul-kayr-nee?'

'Sort of,' Vaibhav replied.

The volunteer nodded and proceeded to the other rows while continually relaying communication to his colleagues over his walkie-talkie.The emcee soon left the stage and the performing band got on and set up the orchestra.

'Get on with it already, Rihanna!' someone screamed from the audience.

Five minutes later, Rihanna obliged. The keyboard offered a cue, and she serenaded the mesmerized audience from backstage with a slow number. Gradually, the spotlight shone on her as she made her way on the stage, looking every inch a celebrity in her golden gown. The crowd erupted in deafening applause and whistles, many of them rising to their feet to get a better glimpse of her.

Vaibhav stayed in his seat and clucked his tongue sympathetically. 'Poor people! We were lucky. We got to see her from this close.' He placed his hand millimetres away from his face.

Nisha nodded. 'Yes, we saw her so clearly!'

The slow track was followed by a series of racy, popular songs that had her spectators almost leaping out of their seats in joy and dance. Around three-fourths of an hour into her performance, the orchestra keyed down their volume and tempo as Rihanna decided to make a short speech about her journey as a singer.

'It has been more than a decade now, and I seem to enjoy it more with every passing day,' she said. 'But with every passing day I also realize this glory is short-lived. For in every nook and corner of the world, you will find an artist waiting to rise and topple you off your high horse. Hence, organizers, please take note and help me make whatever money I can off more such concerts while I've still got the mojo!'

A round of laughter and applause followed. She waited for the din to die down before continuing. 'Modesty is a strange virtue. You lose it the moment you claim to have acquired it. And I, by Jove, have never even claimed to be a modest artist.'

Another round of laughter followed. Vaibhav whispered to Nisha. 'Of course she is not modest. We saw that at the hotel yesterday.'

One of the stage volunteers brought an acoustic guitar and handed it to Rihanna. She strapped it diagonally across her and settled on a chair before continuing to speak. 'But then, God has always had His ways of bringing me down to the ground every time I've allowed your love to get to my head. He shows me someone far more talented than I am, someone I realize I have much to learn from, or someone who helps me remember that big successes begin with baby steps. Something similar happened this morning.'

'Is she only going to talk now?' Vaibhav asked Nisha. 'We might as well leave early then so that we can catch our flight in time tomorrow.'

'Wait, Papa,' Nisha clasped his hand. 'She is not done singing.'

Rihanna went on. 'I made a new little friend from India this morning who handed me a note. I was about to dismiss it as another fan's letter when something made me read it carefully. And you know what? I was blown away by what I read. Written by a girl eleven years of age, it was a song with such simple yet beautiful lyrics that it sent me into a bit of a tizzy.'

Vaibhav turned to Nisha, stone shocked. 'What did she just say?'

Nisha looked at him and grinned ear to ear. 'She said an Indian girl eleven years of age handed her a song she had written!'

Vaibhav was flabbergasted. 'Nisha…is she talking about…'

'Vaibhav Kul-kayr-nee?' the young volunteer was back, kneeling next to them in the aisle. 'Can I have you and your daughter come along with me?'

'What…what happened?' Vaibhav chewed nervously on his moustache.

'You have been requested to come to the green room,' he said. 'We haven't got much time, I'm afraid.'

As a confused father and daughter followed the volunteer down the steps and towards the green room located on the opposite side of the stadium, they overheard Rihanna continue to tell the audience the story of that morning.

'…So, little girl, I understand you are in this audience and I think I have the tacit permission to use your song right here, right now, on stage.' She strummed the guitar. 'And once again, thanks for proving that talent and art see no age, language, and regional barriers. This stage is as much yours, and of the millions like you, as it is mine tonight. I had little time to compose the music, but I guess we will just make do with what I could manage. This is for you, my gorgeous young friend from India!'

Sweaty and completely out of breath, Vaibhav was now in the green room reserved for Rihanna and her band. Nisha stood next to him. He felt her cold, damp hand in his. They looked out through the half-open door of the green room; the stage was now visible from a different and a much closer angle. Rihanna had strummed a few chords and had just begun to sing a song that had clearly never been heard before by her spectators.

'Will someone tell me what's going on?' Vaibhav asked again, his tone a mixture of excitement and restlessness.

The organizer who had played spoilsport to Vaibhav's plans at The Opera House came into the green room with a piece of paper, which he handed to Nisha with a smile. 'I think your father deserves an explanation, kid. Let him know what you've been up to!'

Nisha handed the paper to Vaibhav, her hands trembling with excitement. 'I had taken a tram to The Hyatt this morning while you were asleep. I handed this paper at the reception and requested them to pass it on to her.'

'And Rihanna's manager finally came down and met her,' added the organizer. 'He said she had received the letter and had conveyed her thanks, is that right?'

Nisha nodded. 'Yes. I did not know she read it and liked it too.'

'Of course she did,' the organizer chuckled. 'Or else she would not have been singing it right now in front of fifteen thousand people. Oh by the way, buddy, you owe me a beer for all this! I have worked bloody hard to get you here.'

'I don't understand,' Vaibhav said, dumbfounded.

'So once Rihanna put us to this task, we had to put our heads together, the volunteers and I,' he said, 'to make sure we don't lose you in the crowd. Thankfully we found your names in the online booking system and managed to trace you.'

'Wait!' Vaibhav exclaimed, open-eyed. 'That song,' he said, pointing in the direction of the stage, 'has that song been written by…'

'Read it for yourself, buddy,' the organizer slapped Vaibhav's shoulder and laughed. 'Our families throw us a lot of surprises. Only, some are far more surprising than the others!'

Nisha looked at her father expectantly as he unfolded the piece of paper and read it in quiet solitude. There was a printout that had the lyrics of the said song typed on it. And on top of it was a handwritten note stapled to the printout.

Dear Rihanna Ma'am,

We are sorry for bothering you yesterday. I am a huge fan, and my father brought me here all the way from India so that I could meet you once. But we did not realize you would be busy, and we should not have disturbed you. I was very scared of talking to you when I saw you yesterday. But later I felt bad because I knew my father had tried so hard to make me meet you and speak to you. I am downstairs at the reception right now and I don't want to meet you. But I will be grateful if you can just read my letter once and send in a word that you got my note. Once we go home I will be able to tell my father that I did speak to you finally. He will be very happy.

> *PS: I wrote this song (overleaf) a few months ago. I would love to share it with you. I hope to be able to sing like you one day.*

A giant, ball-shaped tear escaped Vaibhav's eye and landed on her note. He rubbed his eyes and turned to the printout so he could read the song, when the organizer returned to them with a sense of urgency.

'Alright guys, listen up,' he clapped his hands. 'In a minute, our emcee is going to announce the awarding of a memento to Rihanna. One of our volunteers – she is dressed in a black gown – will be walking up to Rihanna with the memento. We want you, kid, to accompany her and then hand the memento to Rihanna. Simple? All good?'

'But…' Nisha muttered nervously.

'No buts…ah, there she is!' the organizer introduced a young woman dressed in a black gown to Nisha. Vaibhav sat in his seat, too shocked to react. 'Gloria, take Nisha with you. Hand her the memento on the stage, and she hands it to Rihanna. Right?'

'Right!' Gloria smiled confidently.

Vaibhav returned to the lyrics of the song, the printout still in his hands.

I am just a little girl with a dream or two,
Of being showered with fandom, and adulation too,
So I sing a story that waits to be heard,
Of a girl, and her wish to soar like a bird.
My verses are short, as is my song,
They take you to a world beyond right and wrong.
They claim no healing miracle except a smile on your face,
As I sing only of hope, which keeps us in a happy place.
I am just a little girl with her head held high,
I have my fears, but a smile should get me by,
So I sing a story that waits to be heard,
Of a girl, and her wish to soar like a bird.

Before Vaibhav could gather his voice to tell her what he thought of the song, the emcee was already on the stage making the announcement. 'That was a fabulous rendition, Rihanna. Now the city council of Melbourne would like to interrupt your marvellous concert for just a few minutes so that we can give you a token of our appreciation for having made time for us this evening.'

'Stay here,' Gloria offered Nisha her free hand; in the other was a silver shield that was to be handed to Rihanna. They waited at the edge of the stage, waiting to be called.

'And it is only befitting,' the emcee added, 'that we ask Rihanna's little friend from India to come along right away and gift this memento to our guest tonight.'

Nisha walked. Her hand was in Gloria's. With ginger steps she moved along the edge of the stage, the image of Rihanna getting clearer with every step. The thunderous applause that reverberated in the open air of The Rod Laver Arena was lost on her. So were the flashes of lights that came off the media's shutterbugs. She stood in stupor before Rihanna and simply muttered, 'Thank you'.

Gloria nudged her and handed her the shield, which she held in her tiny palms as she carefully balanced it before depositing it in Rihanna's hands. Vaibhav looked at her as she stood facing the crowd – his child, a star-struck fan today, a star herself tomorrow. She turned back and looked at him, and was comforted when she saw him peeping through the half-open door of the green room, clapping for her.

'It is I who should thank you.' Nisha turned around, startled by what she heard. The singer knelt down and took the girl in her warm embrace. 'I loved your song. All the best.'

She was guided back into the green room by Gloria. A few feet away from the door, she ran and jumped right into her father's arms. And she squealed and she laughed and she cried, all at once. He made no effort to hold back his tears either.

'I can't believe you wrote that song,' he spoke after a minute.

The emcee took to the microphone again in the meantime. 'We now break for drinks, ladies and gentlemen. Rihanna returns in ten minutes to enchant you some more. Meanwhile, the orchestra has a few stunning sets of music to enthral you with. We will be right back!'

As the orchestra played a karaoke set as a filler, Rihanna strode into the green room. Vaibhav gently placed Nisha down and faced the artist with a bow.

'I thank you from the bottom of my heart, Rihanna madam.'

'You are one crazy man, do you know that?' Rihanna laughed. 'My team told me you had been trying to meet me ever since you set foot in Australia. They told me today about the night outside The Opera House too.'

'I even sent you emails from India, Madam,' he added. 'But you didn't reply.'

She rolled her head back. 'Looks like I have some apologizing to do! Ok, so here I am, standing before you. Your daughter is lovely.'

'Yes, Madam.'

'Thank you, Ma'am,' Nisha nodded with a bow.

'You have been her role model, Madam,' Vaibhav said. 'Since as far back as I can remember.'

Patting Nisha on the head, she smiled. 'You have had an in-house hero beside you all along, girl. Why did you need to seek a role model sitting seven seas across?'

Nisha turned to her father and smiled. His chest swelled with pride. 'Madam, you are too kind.'

'No, I am only honest,' she maintained. 'You, sir, are your daughter's hero. It takes a hero to go the distance to fulfil his child's wish. Do you agree, Nisha?'

Nisha nodded. 'Yes, Ma'am.'

'No Madam, I am a simple man,' his voice trembled with excitement. 'I had never imagined I would travel this far with her. But it was her love for you that got us here. That is the truth.'

'The truth is that every celebrity has a short life of stardom,' Rihanna said. 'Once my life of stardom ends, your daughter and a million others like her will have another star to admire. But you, her father – you are her eternal star. Nobody in the world can ever take your place. So, there!'

He wept with joy. Wiping his tears, he said, 'We won't take any more of your time, Madam. We will leave now. And once again, really sorry for not letting you finish your omelette.'

'Forgiven! Now go!' She chuckled and waved them off.

They walked out of the green room. He led her back towards the entry into the arena.

'Do you really want to go back inside?' she asked him.

'I don't understand her songs anyway,' he said. 'But don't you want to attend the rest of the concert?'

'Um, no,' she said. 'I am done too.'

'Then what do you want to do?'

'Let's go for a walk down to the river,' she said.

They walked down the road to River Yarra, into the blinding night, towards a brighter tomorrow.

When the Heavens Smiled

Ritesh Arora

Sarthak meets Sarangi through a common friend and love blossoms. But when things seem to be falling on track, like a bolt from the blue, Sarangi is diagnosed with a medical condition that leaves her with only three months to live. With no visible solution at hand, nothing but fate seems to be holding power. Explore uncharted realms of life and beyond with Sarthak as he takes it upon himself to alter Sarangi's destiny.

Ritesh is an author and columnist and works as a management consultant with a global business consulting firm.

ISBN: 978-9382665526; Size: 7.75" x 5.1"; Pages: 168; Binding: Paperback.

You are the Best Wife

Ajay Pandey

This is a story of two people with contradictory ideologies who fall in love. This is a true inspiring story of the author and his struggle with life, after his beloved wife left him halfway through their journey. This heart-warming tale of a boy and a girl who never gave up on their love in face of adversities, ends on a bittersweet and poignant note as Ajay comes to terms with the biggest lesson life has to offer.

An engineer by degree, Ajay works in the IT field and loves to read and trek. He has immortalized his life story through this book.

ISBN: 978-9382665540; Size: 7.75" x 5.1"; Pages: 248; Binding: Paperback.

Keeping the Promises

Dhruv Gajjar

Dhruv had almost lost himself when M brought him back to life with her promises. Dying from a dreadful tumour, every night before they went to sleep, she took a portion of his heart and soul as promises. For better or worse, he'd have to keep the promises for the rest of his life. What were those amusing, surprising and painful promises he kept? Can you live and die...both at the same time?

Dhruv is a doctor by profession, and passionate about working on his fitness using advanced bodyweight training and all kinds of sports.

ISBN: 978-9384180072; Size: 7.75" x 5.1"; Pages: 200; Binding: Paperback.

Love on 3 Wheels

Anurag Anand

A young and ambitious girl misplaces a parcel carrying a large amount of cash. She doesn't want to take help from her suitor who seems to have a whole lot of skeletons in his closet. She doesn't want to lose her job either. What can she do?

This is a saga of love, lust, aspirations and trickery that unfolds over a period of three days, propelling those in its midst into an unmindful frenzy.

Anurag holds a Master's degree in business, but loves to read and explore new places. He has ten books to his credit.

ISBN: 978-9382665588; Size: 7.75" x 5.1"; Pages: 168; Binding: Paperback.